I0667736

B-Very Flat
by Margot Kinberg

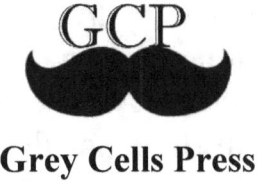

Grey Cells Press

B -Very Flat

Copyright © 2017 by Margot Kinberg

All rights reserved. No part of this publication may be reproduced, distributed, or transmitted in any form or by any means, including photocopying, recording, or other electronic or mechanical methods, without the prior written permission of the author, except in the case of brief quotations embodied in critical reviews and certain other noncommercial uses permitted by copyright law.

This is a work of fiction. Names, characters, businesses, places, events and incidents are either the products of the author's imagination or used in a fictitious manner. Any resemblance to actual persons, living or dead, or actual events is purely coincidental.

Cover art Copyright © 2017 by Lesley Fletcher
Visit http://www.lesleyfletcher.com/ for more information about her work.

Dedication
Like everything I do, this book is dedicated
to my family – you give my life purpose.

Acknowledgements

I have been very fortunate to have the help of many people as I've prepared this book. First, I'd like to thank my family for their strong support. I could not have written this without them in my life. I'd also like to thank Jennifer Shelton for her loyalty, support, careful reading and thoughtful comments. This book is much better for her help.

I've also gotten generous assistance from several people who have given me useful technical information that made this book more authentic. Thanks to Lynn Mancini, not only for her steady and unstinting loyalty and friendship through the years, but also for helpful information about anaphylaxis and epinephrine. Thanks also to Officer Wiley of the Oceanside, CA Police Department for helpful information about police procedures. I'm also grateful to several members of the Oceanside business community for their expertise on video surveillance, record keeping and theft prevention.

Many thanks also to Lesley Fletcher, whose artwork brings the cover of this book alive.

Table of Contents

Chapter One 6

Chapter Two 32

Chapter Three 55

Chapter Four.......................... 78

Chapter Five 102

Chapter Six.......................124

Chapter Seven......................144

Chapter Eight.......................167

Chapter Nine.......................199

Chapter Ten.......................218

Chapter Eleven.......................243

Chapter Twelve.......................269

Chapter Thirteen.......................288

Chapter Fourteen..................... .309

Chapter Fifteen.......................323

Chapter One

Serena Brinkman smiled as she took a deep breath of the crisp October air. The walk between her dormitory and Lessner Hall, the music building, was one of her favorites, especially on sunny, cool mornings like this one. Serena wanted to spend an hour or so practicing her violin before her eleven o'clock Music Theory II class, so she resisted the temptation to sit for a while on one of the benches that lined the cobbled paths around the Tilton University campus. It wasn't easy, though. Like many campuses, Tilton looked its best on sunny autumn days; it was no wonder that most of the publicity pictures of the campus were taken between the end of September and the beginning of November.

When she got to the main entrance to Lessner Hall, Serena stepped inside and paused to put down her violin case and take off her corduroy jacket. She tossed the jacket on her shoulder, picked up her case and turned towards the stairs leading to the basement-level practice rooms. Coming up the stairs was Tony Ferguson, a photographer on the staff of *Vintage*, Tilton's yearbook. As he saw her, Ferguson's face lit up.

"Hi, Serena! Glad I caught you. I've been trying to get hold of you for a couple of days now."

"Sorry, Tony, it's been a busy week."

Serena remembered with embarrassment that Tony had left her two voice mails this week. He wanted to include her in a special mid-year magazine that the *Vintage* staff had decided to put together. The focus of the magazine was to be on Tilton students and faculty who had won special awards or recognition, as well as those who showed particular promise in their fields. Serena had met Tony two weeks earlier after a performance by the university's string ensemble, where she'd had a short solo. Tony had been there to photograph the ensemble, and had been impressed with her playing. He'd been even more impressed with the fact that Serena was a sophomore, since usually only juniors or seniors were selected for solos. After the performance, he'd sought her out and tried to convince her to be profiled in the magazine.

Now, he said, "I hope you're not going to back out on me."

"To be honest, Tony, I really don't think I'm the kind of person you're looking for. That magazine you told me about is supposed to be focused on people who've won major awards, right? That's not me."

"It's also focused on people with real talent, like you. We've got a whole section called, 'People to Watch,' and you'd be perfect for it. I've been doing some background research on you, Serena. You're already taking advanced classes, you're doing solos, and you've got a performance scholarship. I'd say that makes for a pretty impressive profile."

Serena wasn't sure how to respond. Certainly she was flattered that they'd want to profile her for the *Vintage*. She was also aware that she had a lot of talent; you didn't last long as a performance major if you didn't have faith in your own ability. She knew, too, that being profiled might help convince her patrician parents that she'd made the right decision to attend Tilton instead of a more prestigious school like Julliard. Still, she knew of a lot of other people who were just as talented, and she wasn't sure whether she wanted to be featured in a magazine, at least not now in her career.

After a moment, Tony broke the silence. "Come on, Serena, it won't take long, and it'd be good publicity, wouldn't it? Don't

you want a career in music? You'll get
people to notice you a lot more quickly if
you've got write-ups."

"All right, all right," Serena sighed. "I have
to practice now, and then I have an eleven
o'clock class. Then I've got other classes
and things later today, so it'll have to be
tomorrow."

"That's fine. How about we have lunch
together and do the interview part, and then
set up a time for the photography part."

"OK, that'll work."

"Great! Noon tomorrow at the Kozy
Korner?"

"Got it."

Tony watched as Serena turned to go on her
way. From the time he'd met her, he'd been
attracted to her. Now, he was finally going
to get to do something about it. For two
weeks Tony had been haunted by Serena's
burnished black hair, pale, heart-shaped face
and clear blue eyes. Her musical ability and
her intense concentration when she was
playing only made her more appealing. With
a smile, he shrugged his backpack off his
shoulders and fumbled for the spiral
notebook he always carried. When he found
it, he pulled it out and wrote the words
Serena - Kozy Korner – noon on the cover.
He tossed the notebook into his backpack

and headed to the *Vintage*'s small office in the Student Union building.

Finally free of Tony, Serena made her way down to the basement level of the building. Lessner Hall's basement level was a long, L-shaped corridor, lined on both sides with practice rooms. At each end of the corridor was a larger room for orchestra, ensemble and band practices. Serena passed several of the smaller rooms on her way to her favorite. From the rooms came the sound of various instruments. As she reached her favorite practice room, Serena saw a girl coming out of the room next door.
"Hi, Serena."
"Oh, hi, Michelle."

Michelle Park was also a performance major; in fact, she was one of the most talented violinists in the country, and had had her choice of several world-class music schools. Her family's financial situation had placed most of them out of her reach, but Tilton had offered her scholarship money and besides, it was less expensive than other schools with high-quality music programs. Interestingly enough, although Tilton's music program wasn't as well-known as, say, Julliard's, Tilton graduates seemed to go on to highly successful music careers.

Michelle and her family had liked what they'd heard and read about the success rate of Tilton's alumnae. Also, Michelle's family had wanted her to attend a school in a smaller town where they thought she would be safer.

Although they were rivals, Serena respected Michelle's drive and talent. In her mind, Michelle motivated her to do better. Serena had had an easy time in her high school's music program; now that she was in college, she was finding out what real competition was like. So far, she hadn't been able selected yet as concertmistress for any of the Tilton orchestra's performances, although she'd competed for it twice. Michelle had won both competitions, but Serena had been given positive feedback and a spot in the first violin section. She hoped that if she kept practicing, she would do better.
Now Serena asked, "Getting your 'music workout' in before Theory?"
"It's the best time of day to get a good room," answered Michelle. "The competition for the tour ensemble is next week, and I'm not ready yet."
"I'm not, either," admitted Serena ruefully.

Both girls were scheduled to compete for concertmistress in the Young Artists'

Orchestra, a group that comprised the best musicians from several local colleges and universities. This orchestra made an annual tour of several large Eastern cities. The tour was a golden opportunity to travel, to get a sense of life as a performer, and most importantly, to get noticed by professional orchestras. Every student musician took this competition very seriously, and most had been practicing for months. Serena knew that she wouldn't have a chance, especially against someone as talented as Michelle, unless she used every minute of free time to get ready. With a smile, she said "Well, guess I'd better use the room while I've got it."

"I'll see you later, then."

"OK."

With that, Serena went into the practice room, turned on the light, and got ready to play. Briskly, she opened up her backpack, pulled out the sheet music for the piece that she wanted to use for the jury, and placed it on the music stand. Then, she lovingly took her violin out of her case, rosined the bow and set to work.

As Serena began to practice, Michelle quickly walked down the hall and, when she reached the staircase, headed upstairs and towards one of the large, comfortable chairs in the main lobby of the building. She put down her violin case and pulled her PDA out of her backpack. She hastily scanned her obligations for the day, and pulled absently at her hair as she wondered how she would be able to meet all of them. Michelle carried a full load of courses, practiced for hours each day, and worked part-time at the local FreshNow grocery store. She rarely dated, since her traditional Korean family discouraged her from getting into relationships. It was, in fact, her family that was the biggest source of stress in Michelle's life right now. Her parents had made it quite clear that she must work as hard as necessary to win the competition for the annual tour, and Michelle wasn't sure she could face them if she failed. Simply put, they wanted her to be the best, and would be satisfied with nothing less.

Michelle realized that her chief competition for first violin for the Young Artists' Orchestra would be Serena Brinkman. In a way, she was sorry about that; she liked Serena, and certainly respected her musical ability. That didn't matter, though, when it came to winning. For Michelle, the stakes in this competition were far too high for her to think about how much she liked and respected Serena. If she lost the competition, Michelle knew that she would alienate her family. She might even have to drop out of Tilton, since her parents had let her know that they would only support her education if she made the most of it; to them, that meant winning. With a worried glance at the time displayed on her PDA, Michelle tossed it quickly back into her backpack, zipped it up, and hurried to her class in Advanced Ear Training.

An hour and a half later, Serena finished her practice session and took the elevator to the third floor of Lessner Hall. Once there, she went into the first classroom on the right, where Professor Jesse Montgomery was getting ready to teach his Music Theory II class. Serena liked Dr. Montgomery; she'd taken his introductory Music Theory course last spring and felt that she'd learned a lot. While she wasn't as interested in the history of music as Dr. Montgomery was, she liked his teaching style and hoped to take his History of Instruments course next year. She knew he had an interest in antique instruments, and guessed that he'd make the course exciting. Now, she slid into her seat and pulled a notebook out of her backpack as Montgomery inserted a CD into the classroom's technology center.

[14]

When class ended, Serena stopped at Montgomery's desk. "Do you have a minute, Professor Montgomery?" she asked.

"Sure, Serena. Do you have a question for me?"

"Well, no. I have something to show you."

"All right, let's see it."

Serena leaned down and opened her violin case. Out came her prize, the sight of which made Montgomery catch his breath.

"Oh, my God! It's a genuine Amati!"

"That's right. I usually don't bring it anywhere with me, because I don't want it stolen. But you were telling me about your paper on old violins, and I know you're interested in antiques, so I thought I would show you mine."

"Where did you get it?"

"It was in my family for a long time. I actually don't know how we first got it – probably one of my robber-baron ancestors," Serena said with a smile. "When I turned out to be a violin player, my grandfather said I would appreciate it the most, so he gave it to me."

"You're a lucky young lady!"

"Thanks. I love having it, even though I don't play it much. I usually play my other violin. I save this one for special performances. I just brought it today to show it to you."

"You should really be careful about where you keep it."

"Oh, I am. I keep it locked up in my dorm's valuables safe when I'm not using it."

"Smart girl." Then, after a pause, Montgomery said, "Would you mind if I tried it for a moment."

"All right; I need to go to another class, but I have a few minutes."

Serena handed the violin to Montgomery, whose eyes glowed with appreciation behind his horn-rimmed glasses. Tenderly, he tucked it under his chin and played a few notes. After a few moments, he reluctantly returned the instrument to Serena.

"Thank you so much for showing this to me."

"Oh, you're welcome. I thought you might like to see it." Then, after a quick glance at her watch, Serena said, "I had no idea what time it was getting to be. I've got to go – sorry. See you in class."

Absently, Montgomery nodded and said, "OK, see you next time." As Serena placed the violin gently back into its case, he said, "Be careful of that. Someone might take it."

"I will, don't worry."

Serena turned and left the classroom. Montgomery stared after her, his eyes never leaving the violin case that she carried. Ever since he could remember, he'd loved violins and violin music. Although he didn't have the world-class talent required to perform in international orchestras and competitions, he played whenever he could. His main interest, though, was music in the abstract, and the ways that instruments were constructed and used to create different sound effects. To Jesse Montgomery, there was no more perfect violin music than the music that came from an Amati. He couldn't believe that someone as young and inexperienced as Serena Brinkman could play one whenever she wanted; he doubted she knew how lucky she was.

By five-thirty, Serena had finished her day's classes and returned to Lessner Hall for another practice session. Now, she was making her way through the deepening twilight back to Cooper Hall, her dormitory, where she wanted to pick up her mail, drop off her books, and lock up her violin before dinner. When she got to the building, she went first to the main floor, where she carefully locked her violin in the dorm's safe. Then, as she walked up to the bank of mailboxes on the ground floor of the dormitory, she saw Marcie Bratton, her RA. Marcie was a strawberry blond, freckle-faced junior who was majoring in military science. She was very active in Tilton's R.O.T.C. program and hoped for a military career.

"Hey, Marcie!"

"Oh, hi, Serena. How's it going?"

"OK, thanks, just busy."

"I hear that! C'mon, I'll walk up to the floor with you."

"Sounds good."

The two girls went to the third floor, where their rooms were only a few doors apart. Serena felt lucky that Marcie was the R.A. for her floor. Marcie's military training helped her to keep order. At the same time, she was friendly, and always made the time for anyone who needed some advice or a sympathetic ear. When they got to their floor, Marcie said, "Got big plans for tonight?"

"No, just getting some dinner, and then off to the library. I have a big chem. exam tomorrow."

"Good luck!"

"Thanks."

"Hey, you need someone to go over your stuff with you? I aced chem. last year."

"No, thanks. Patricia's going to help me. She's in the same class."

"OK, see you later."

"See you."

Serena went to her own room, dropped her mail on her bed and put her backpack on her desk chair. She opened it and fished a notebook out of it. Then, she scrounged around on her desk until she found a pen that worked. She had just finished organizing herself when she heard a knock at her partially open door. She turned around to see Patricia Stanley, a blue-eyed blonde, standing in the doorway.

"Come on in," Serena said.

"Are you ready, or what?"

"I'm ready. Let's go."

The two girls left Serena's room, pulling the door shut as they went. Then, they walked to the elevator. After Serena had pushed the button, Patricia said, "You must be miles away. You haven't said more than a word to me."

"Oh – sorry. Yeah, I have been preoccupied."

"The competition – right?"

"Exactly! It's a week away and I'm not ready."

"You will be. Promise."

With that Patricia leaned over and kissed
Serena, then smiled. "I know you'll get first
chair. You're the best."
"No, you are, for being such a support."
Serena returned Patricia's kiss as the
elevator finally arrived.

Patricia had been an important part of
Serena's life for almost two years. A native
of Southern California, Patricia had chosen
Tilton because she wanted to leave the
heavy traffic and high rents of her native
Malibu Canyon. Besides, her interest was
law enforcement, and she hoped to become a
detective, but she didn't want to work for
any of the local police departments, or for
the California State Police. She also wanted
the chance to try life on her own, away from
her somewhat overprotective software-
developer father and commercial artist
stepmother. They'd wanted her to attend a
nearby college and then settle near them.
Patricia, though, had other plans. So she
and her family had struck a bargain: her
father and stepmother would support her
choice of a school that was in a different
part of the country, so long as she chose a
school in a relatively small town, away
from the larger dangers posed by big cities.
They'd settled on Tilton when it was
discovered that friends of Patricia's father

had sent their son there successfully, and when Patricia had found out that Tilton Criminal Justice graduates seemed to go on to successful careers. There was a very high post-graduation employment rate from the Department of Criminal Justice, and that appealed to the entire Stanley family.

Patricia and Serena had met when their families had gone on the same Caribbean cruise two and a half years before. At first, Patricia hadn't thought she and Serena would get along. Serena came from a family whose roots were deeply entrenched in Philadelphia's Main Line – very different from Patricia's own middle class-made good upbringing. Much to both girls' surprise, though, they'd hit it off almost at once. After the cruise, the two girls had kept in touch and shared visits to each other's homes. Before long, they'd fallen in love. When Patricia was accepted into the Criminal Justice program at Tilton, Serena had joined her there. In fact, Serena had turned down several offers to attend world-class schools of music so that she could study at the same school as Patricia. The two were planning a future together, although neither was sure exactly what that future would be. At nineteen years old, they had time.

Now, they walked slowly towards the Student Center, enjoying the crisp evening air. As they strolled, Patricia said, "So, what do you want to do this weekend?"

"I'm not sure I'll have a lot of free time. I got an Email this morning from Troy. He wants to visit this weekend. Of course, you're welcome to hang with us."

"That could be fun. I like your cousin." Troy Brinkman was Serena's cousin, the only child of her father's brother. He was a junior at Millworth College, a select liberal-arts college an hour west of Tilton.

"Yeah, it should be fun. I'm thinking he might like to go to Harvest Day. You interested?"

"Sure, I guess, if you want to make the time for it."

Harvest Day was Tilton's annual fall party, which was held at a nearby farm owned by Tilton's School of Agriculture. Events included outdoor races and games, tours of the farm and barn, a costume contest and later, a bonfire and dance. Serena and Patricia had gone last year and enjoyed themselves. They hadn't yet decided whether to attend this year, mostly because Serena wanted to spend as much time as possible preparing for the tour group competition.

Serena said, "I know I need to practice. In fact, I'm really stressing about it, but I don't want to miss Harvest Day, and I don't want to say 'No' to Troy. He doesn't get a lot of free time."

"Well, let's plan on it then. We can take the shuttle bus out to the farm, and then we won't have to worry about parking."

"OK, I'll Email Troy. For now, though, let's focus on food!" The two girls had reached the Student Union, and both were eager to find a place to sit and get their dinner before the cafeteria became too crowded.

Tilton's Student Union building had three places to eat: a large cafeteria (one of three on campus), the Kozy Korner Kafe, a smaller grill, and the Pit Stop, which served fountain drinks, coffee and prepackaged sandwiches and snacks. When they reached the building, Serena and Patricia joined the rapidly-expanding line at the entrance to the cafeteria. When their turn came, each girl showed her university identification to the cafeteria attendant, and then they scanned the buffet.

"Oh, good!" Patricia said, "No mystery meat tonight!"

Serena laughed, "Thank God! If I see one more thing labeled "patty," I think I'm going to give up eating forever."

After selecting trays, utensils and plates, the two girls walked through the buffet line. They soon were served with grilled chicken, rolls and salads, and made their way to a table. As they sat down, Serena said, "I'm glad it's not spaghetti tonight, either. I love the smell of it, and it always makes me mad that I can't eat it. There's just too much risk of peanut flour in the sauce."

"I know," said Patricia. Serena had told her quite a while ago about her violent allergy to peanuts and peanut dust. As long as Serena didn't ingest anything with peanuts in it, all was well, but there was a long list of foods that often contained peanuts or some peanut product, so she always had to be very careful of what she ate. With Serena, anaphylactic shock was an ever-present risk.

As the two girls began to eat, their conversation turned to the chemistry exam they would face the next day. Patricia was much the better science student, and felt more or less prepared; she was hoping, though, that by helping Serena, she'd get have an even better chance of remembering what had been covered in class. Their professor was not known for leniency, and this was to be a cumulative midterm. Serena was just reaching into her backpack for her chemistry notebook when a voice from behind her interrupted her.

"Hi, Serena."
"Oh, hi, Tony. Patricia, this is Tony Ferguson, the photographer that I was telling you about. The one from the *Vintage*."
After the introductions had been made, Tony slid into a seat.
"Mind if I join you?"
"Uh, sure, yeah, I guess," Serena said uncertainly. She slowly put her notebook back into her backpack, a little irritated at having to change the subject of conversation. She was worried about the chemistry test, and had really hoped to focus on it.
Tony nodded his thanks, and the three students turned their attention to their dinner. As they ate, they talked about the inedible cafeteria food, Harvest Day and the profiles Tony was doing for the *Vintage*.

When they'd finished, they took their trays to the large dish rack, where dishes were left until they were taken to the dishwashing room for cleaning. They threw their trash away and then prepared to leave.
"So, what are you guys doing?" Tony asked hopefully.

"We're off to the library to study for a major chem exam," Serena answered, hoping he would take her hint and leave.

"Oh, OK, well, I guess I'll see you tomorrow then."

"Yeah, see you then."

With that, Serena and Patricia headed down the path that led from the Student Union building across campus to the library. Serena was relieved to see that Tony wasn't following them. She liked him well enough, but the more she thought about it, the more she was convinced that she had no chance of passing that exam without a lot of help. She wanted to concentrate on work, not conversation. Soon, the two girls had reached Sheaffer Memorial Library, an imposing brick-and-glass building that boasted two large computer labs, hundreds of thousands of books in print, and a an equally impressive electronic collection. The library was a favorite haunt for students who were preparing for exams, because it also had several small-group workrooms and two comfortable lounges. Knowing her tendency to procrastinate when it came to chemistry, Serena said, "I guess we'd better pick a workroom. I will never focus if we go to a lounge."

"OK, workroom it is."

The two girls settled in the first empty workroom they found, and before long, the table in the room was covered with open books, scrawled lecture notes and scattered equations written on sheets of notepaper. For the next two hours, Patricia patiently went over the last few weeks' worth of work with Serena. Finally, she asked, "OK, does this make sense now?"

"Yes, believe it or not, it finally does. I don't know how you did it, but I finally get it."

"You're not stupid, Serena, you just need to get a handle on a few things."

"Maybe, but you're also a good tutor. Look, if it's OK with you, I want to get back to the dorm. I need to work on my Music Theory paper, and if I have the energy, I want to practice for an hour."

"OK, I have to catch up on my Email, anyway."

With that, Serena and Patricia refilled their backpacks, zipped up their jackets and prepared to return to Cooper Hall. When they arrived at the dormitory, Serena said jokingly, "Here's my stop."

"I'll walk you upstairs."

"OK."

The two girls took the elevator to the third floor and headed down the hall to where

Serena shared a room with Tessa Oliver, a sophomore math major. There, Patricia said, "Meet you for breakfast?"

"Got it. Eight-thirty at the caf, right?"

"Right. See ya."

"See ya." With that, Patricia gave Serena a brief kiss, and turned to go back to the elevators as Serena unlocked her door and went into her room. As she turned, Patricia almost collided with Marcie Bratton, who was on her way to Serena and Tessa's room.

"Whoops! Sorry, Marcie. Didn't see you."

"No problem."

Patricia smiled, "See you."

"Yeah, see you around."

Marcie watched Patricia steadily as she turned and went back to the elevator. Then, she shook her head and tapped on Serena's door.

"Come in."

"Hi, Serena."

"Oh, hi, Marcie"

"You doing OK? You ready for that chem. exam?"

"Yeah, I think so. Patricia's a real help to me."

"That's good. Any time you get stuck, just remember I'm right down the hall."

"OK, thanks."

"Oh, and I wanted to remind you about the floor meeting tomorrow night at eight. Are you going to be there?"

"I have it written down, thanks."

"Good. Uh, Serena?"

Serena looked up at Marcie's change of tone.

"Yeah?"

"Look, it's none of my business, but… well, this thing with Patricia. Are you sure it's such a good idea?"

"What do you mean?"

"Well, you know. People can be pretty cruel. You sure you want to be so, well, obvious?"

"It's the 21st century, Marcie! People can think what they want, but Patricia and I are together, and people are just going to have to deal with it. Why, has somebody been saying something?"

"Well, no. It's just that I don't want you to be hurt."

"We're fine, Marcie. Really. But thanks for caring."

"OK, well, just thought I'd stick my nose in. That's what RAs do," Marcie said with a mechanical smile.

"And I appreciate that you care about us."

"Well, I'll let you get back to your practicing."

"Thanks. See ya."

"See ya."

As Marcie left the room, Serena turned her attention back to the violin she'd pulled out of its case. After almost an hour of practice, she put the violin away. Then, she turned reluctantly to her desktop computer, and to the Music Theory paper she'd put off for too long already. By eleven-thirty, she'd finished her first draft, and realized that if she didn't get some sleep, she wouldn't be able to concentrate the next day. So she shut down her computer and rummaged in the top drawer of her dresser for her toothbrush, toothpaste and skin cleanser. She went down the hall to the large bathroom, and went in. Inside, she saw her roommate.

"Hi, Tessa. I didn't know you'd gotten back."

"Yeah, our prof. let us out early, so I decided to just get some food and then come back. I hate night classes."

"Me, too. Fortunately, I haven't had any this year."

"Don't rub it in."

Serena turned towards the sink she'd chosen, washed her face and brushed her teeth. Then, she and Tessa walked back to their room. Once there, Tessa glanced over at Serena's desk and said, "Hey, Serena, your phone's flashing."

"Thanks."

Serena picked up her cell phone and noticed that she had a text message. She opened it and read the message: *See you tomorrow at noon. Tony.* With an irritated sigh, she deleted the message and put the phone back on her desk.

"What's the matter?"

"Oh, nothing. Just some guy from the *Vintage* who wants to interview me. I wish he'd leave me alone."

"What? Sick of your fans already?" Tessa asked mockingly.

"Shut up!" Serena said playfully and threw a pillow across the room at her roommate. Tessa returned the pillow with just as much force, and then the two girls settled for the night.

Chapter Two

Troy Brinkman clicked the "end call" button on his cell phone with a shaking hand. This was the third time today that the loan company had called, and he was getting nervous. This last time, they'd even talked about a lawsuit. It had all started innocently enough, or so it had seemed to Troy. Like his cousin Serena, he'd come from a privileged background, and had always had the best of everything: the best private schools, expensive summer camps and private lessons. He'd done well in school, and had decided he was interested in a career in finance. His parents had wanted him to attend the University of Pennsylvania's Wharton School of Business. Instead, he'd chosen Millworth, since several of his friends were planning to go there. It hadn't been easy to convince his parents to send him to Millworth, but Troy had been glad of his choice.

The trouble had started when one of his friends had introduced him to internet gambling. At first, Troy had been excited by the games, and, since he was good at strategy, he'd done fairly well. Soon, though, he'd started to lose money. Before long, he'd spent all of the money his parents had given him for expenses, and started using money from the trust fund his grandfather had set up for him. It didn't take long for that to be gone, too, and then Troy had gotten desperate. He'd taken out several loans and was now ten thousand dollars in debt. He knew that he wouldn't get any help from his parents. Once before, they'd caught him forging his father's name to a check. They'd told him then that if he got into trouble like that again, he would be on his own. Troy's father, especially, wanted his son to be an independent, responsible adult, and had made it clear he wouldn't coddle Troy.

Now, Troy stared at his cell phone for a moment, and then put it back in his pocket. He was going to have to figure out something to do, and soon, about his debt. The finance company representative had told him that if he didn't pay the debt within thirty days, they would start legal proceedings. He hadn't made a payment for almost six months, and they wouldn't wait much longer. No time to think about it now, though. He had to get to his Managerial Accounting class, and then he had another class. After that, he planned to pack and head east to Tilton, to visit Serena for the weekend. He was looking forward to the visit. He'd always gotten along very well with Serena, and not even his financial plight was going to keep him stuck in his room all weekend.

While Troy was struggling with his debt problems, Serena was facing a struggle of her own. The chemistry exam had been harder than she'd anticipated, and it had taken her almost the entire class period to go through the problems. There wouldn't be much opportunity to go over her work before the proctor called time. She snuck a quick glance over at Patricia, who was chewing the end of her pencil as she reviewed her own exam. Anxiously, Serena turned her attention back to her own paper and frantically tried to go over as many of the problems as she could. Too soon, the proctor said, "Time's up, everyone. Please put your pencils down and pass your work forward."

After handing in their papers, Serena and Patricia met at the classroom door. "Was that awful, or what?" Patricia asked as they the left the room.
"I thought it was just me!"
"No, that test was horrible! Want to go drown our sorrows in a latte?"

"I wish I could. I have to meet that guy from the *Vintage*, though. I told him I'd meet him at noon at the Kozy Korner. You want to come?"

"Nah, this is your show. Besides, I really should do my laundry. I'm almost out of clean underwear. And then I have a heavy date with a nap."

Serena giggled, "Well, we all have our priorities. I'll call you later, OK?"

"Yup."

With that, Patricia turned to go back to her dormitory, which was across the campus' main courtyard from Cooper Hall, where Serena lived. Serena, in turn, went in the opposite direction towards the Student Union building.

When she got there, she headed towards the Kozy Korner. She pushed open the door, and saw that Tony Ferguson was already there, sitting in a booth nursing a soda. He waved to her and pointed towards the empty seat facing him. Serena nodded and was soon at the table. "Mind if I leave my backpack here while I order?"

"Sure, go ahead."

In a few moments, Serena had returned to the table with a tuna sandwich, a bag of chips and a soda of her own. "OK," she said. "I'm ready. Fire away."

Tony had wanted to chat first, but Serena was clearly in a hurry. No matter; he could come to his real purpose later.

"OK, first, tell me about your background."

"Well, I'm from Devon, Pennsylvania. I –"

" – nice area!"

"Yeah, it is. Anyway, I'm an only child. My dad's a financial consultant, and my mom has her real estate license. She doesn't really do a lot with it, though. She's more into her clubs and charities."

"I get the idea. How did you get interested in the violin?"

"Well, I always loved music. My mom tells me I started pretending to play instruments when I was a toddler. Don't print that!!"

"Don't worry, the point of this isn't to embarrass you. Go on."

"OK. So my parents gave me violin lessons starting when I was four, and I've played ever since."

"So why did you choose Tilton?"

Serena had thought about admitting that her most important reason for being at Tilton was Patricia. In the end, she decided that might sound too silly and sentimental. So she satisfied herself by answering, "Tilton's got a great reputation in the music world, and it's not too far from home, without being too close. Besides, I have a scholarship."

"I heard about that. Music scholarships aren't easy to get! So, what are your plans after college?"

"I'm hoping to join a nationally ranked orchestra like the New York Philharmonic or even the Philadelphia Orchestra."

"Ever thought of teaching music?"

"Me? No. I don't have the patience for it."

"You're in the competition for the Young Artists' Orchestra, right?"

"Right. That's next week."

"Are you ready?"

"I will be."

Tony could see that Serena was getting a bit restive. She'd been eating her lunch as they talked, and was now nearly finished. He'd even caught her peeking at her watch a few times. He realized that if he didn't make a move now, there might not be another chance. So, taking a breath, he said, "Listen, Serena. I – I was wondering. Are you busy tonight?"

Serena looked up, her blue eyes widened in surprise. "Tony, are you asking me out?"

"If you're interested."

"Look," Serena said, suddenly a little embarrassed, "I like you, but, well, I'm in a relationship with someone."

Tony lowered his head a little and muttered,
"I guess I shouldn't be surprised at that.
Forget it, OK? No big deal."
"No problem. Uh, I better go."
"Sure, yeah. Thanks for the interview. Oh,
about the photograph…"
"Oh, yeah, how does that work?"
"Well, the good equipment's kept in the
Vintage office. Could you stop by there
later? Then, we can get a good camera and
find a spot."
"I guess so. What time?"
"How about three? It's still light enough for
a good shot then."
"All right. I'll see you then."
"Later."

Serena put her dishes and napkin on her tray
and carried it to the trashcan next to the
door. She dumped the trash, placed the tray
on the shelf top of the trashcan and left the
restaurant. All of a sudden, she was
beginning to feel a little uncomfortable
around Tony Ferguson. She hadn't realized
he was interested in her. That was going to
make doing this profile awkward, but at
least the interview part was over. A couple
of pictures and she could forget about it.
That, at least, was a comfort. Besides, there
wasn't any time now to think about Tony.

She had to get over to Lessner Hall and practice for a while before her next class.

Michelle Park had been practicing in the basement of Lessner Hall since ten o'clock, preparing the piece she was planning to play for the tour group competition. She was almost satisfied with her work, but it never hurt to practice one more time. Besides, a less than perfect performance wouldn't get her selected for the orchestra, and her playing still needed a little more polishing. So, after a brief trip to the restroom, she was returning to the practice room when she happened to notice that Serena Brinkman was in a nearby room. Michelle decided to pause and listen to her competition. What she heard left her surprised and dismayed. Serena was playing brilliantly. Michelle's trained ear and sense of music told her that Serena was going to be a formidable rival. Suddenly afraid for her own position as Tilton's finest violinist, Michelle hurried back to her own practice room. Aggressively, she flipped her sheet music to the beginning of the piece, then tucked her violin under her chin and began the piece again. As she played, her mind raced as she contemplated what would happen if she lost this competition. Angry with herself for losing her focus, she shook her head, took a deep breath and started again.

When Serena finished her practice session, she decided to stop upstairs at the office of her advisor, Dr. Sergei Berzin. Berzin had been concertmaster for a Russian orchestra for twenty years before his health had forced him to retire from active performances. He'd come to the United States after the fall of the Soviet Union, and had settled comfortably into life at Tilton, where he'd been lured by the relatively low cost of living and easy pace of life. At fifty-eight, he was no longer interested in big-city living or hectic traveling and performance schedules. He was content to mentor the next generation of musicians. He was highly demanding, but Serena didn't mind that. She knew her playing would be better if she were pushed. Now, she tapped on the doorframe of his open office. "Do you have a minute, Dr. Berzin?"

"For you, Serena, yes, I do."

"Thanks. I want to be really ready for Wednesday's jury. Do you think you could listen to my piece and coach me?"

"Of course. Now, impress me," Berzin said with a smile. He settled into his chair and waited while Serena drew out her sheet music and placed it on the music stand

Berzin kept in his office. Then, she lifted out her violin and bow, and began to play. As she played, Berzin listened closely. It was his habit to let his students play through a piece completely before he gave feedback. When Serena finished, Berzin said, "That is very good, Serena. You have the music exactly right. Now all you need is passion. Push yourself and really feel what you are playing."

"Do you think I can win the competition?"

"You will have to work hard. There are other very, very good students. But yes, I think you can."

"Thanks. I hope so, but you're right. There are some really good students who are going to compete."

"Do not worry about them. Worry only about your own playing. Focus on that and you will do better."

"I'll try."

Serena thanked Berzin for his time, and then packed up her violin, bow and sheet music, and shrugged her backpack onto her shoulders. As she left Berzin's office, she saw Jesse Montgomery heading into his own office next door. "Oh, hi, Dr. Montgomery."

"Hi, Serena. I just heard your piece; you're really doing well."

"Thanks, I'm trying to."

"Not got your Amati with you today?"

"No, I leave that at the dorm safe."

"Of course. That's wise of you. Will you be using it for the competition? You're scheduled to compete for concertmistress, right?"

"Right. And yes, I think I will use it for the competition – just for luck."

"If you're going to do that, you should practice with it before you actually compete, just to make sure you have the feel of it. Every violin's different."

"That makes sense. Thanks."

Montgomery nodded and then, holding up a finger, hurried over to answer his telephone, which had begun to ring. Serena shook her head, pointed at her watch and waved to indicate that she had to leave. Montgomery nodded again and waved in return. Then Serena left his office, hoping she'd have time to get back to Cooper Hall and leave her backpack and violin before it was time to meet Tony Ferguson at the *Vintage* office.

By the time Troy Brinkman had gotten out of class and packed his things for the weekend, it was already nearly three. He was eager to get on the road so that he could get to Tilton in time to get settled and take Serena to dinner. Troy and Serena had been friends as well as cousins since childhood, and he was looking forward to spending time with her. He hadn't seen her just lately, and it would be good to catch up. Besides, he was eager for anything to take his mind off his troubles. He gave a final glance at the contents of his overnight bag, zipped it up, and slung it on his shoulder. Then, he sent Serena a text message to let her know he was on his way. He glanced around at his room to make sure he had everything he needed and slammed the door shut. He took the stairs to the ground floor of his dormitory and quickly got into his Lexus. At least he hadn't had to sell that yet. He tossed his luggage in the back seat and was soon headed east on winding country roads towards Tilton.

On my way: see you in a little over an hour said the message on Serena's cell phone screen. She smiled as she replied, *'bout time, lazy!* and flipped her phone shut. Then she turned her attention back to Tony Ferguson, who was showing her around the *Vintage*'s small, cramped office on the second floor of the Student Union building.
"...and this is where we do the press run," Tony concluded as he pointed towards a large machine in the back of the room. "You guys do a beautiful job, too."

"Thanks. OK, so you ready?"

"I guess so. What do I do?"

"Let me do the work. We'll find a good spot where the light's right, and then just get a few shots."

"I can handle that, I guess."

"Of course you can."

Tony slid open the bottom drawer of a locked, battered file cabinet, and pulled out a camera. He looked at it carefully to be sure it was the one he wanted. Then, nodding briskly, he slid the drawer shut and locked the cabinet again. Then, he swung the camera's strap onto his shoulder and said, "OK, let's go." The two young people left the office and took the staircase to the ground floor of the building, zipped up their jackets, and went outside. After a short walk, they got to a courtyard that separated the Student Union building from the Administration building. There, several benches, a water fountain and some strategically-planted trees made for an attractive backdrop.

"Sit on the bench right there, and I'll do the rest," said Tony.

"OK." Serena sat down awkwardly.

"Relax. It's only a picture. It won't hurt."

Serena laughed a little at her self-consciousness. "I'm just not used to my own photo spread," she joked.

"OK, look over here.

One.....two....three.... smile!" Tony said as he snapped the picture. He took three or four more shots, with Serena facing in different directions. Then, satisfied he'd gotten some good pictures, he said, "I guess that's it."

"That wasn't bad at all."

"Yeah... uh...hey, you want to get a soda or coffee or something?"

"Tony, I'm sorry, but I told you earlier. I'm with someone."

"No, no no! This is strictly business. Really."

"Well..." Serena sighed, "OK, I guess so. My cousin's coming for the weekend, and he'll be here in about half an hour, but I have time for coffee."

"Good."

Tony packed up his camera, and then he and Serena returned to the Student Union and went up one flight of stairs, where the Pit Stop was located. Each ordered a coffee, and they took seats at the bright-orange barstools that were the Pit Stop's only seating.

Awkwardly, Tony said, "You take a good picture."

"Thanks, I think."

[45]

"No, I mean it. I think we got some good shots."

"I'm glad."

"So you're really going out with someone?"

"Yes, I am. We've been dating for almost two years."

"Going to get married?"

"I don't know about that. I'm only nineteen."

"Well, you're not married now, right? Why not go out to dinner with me? I'm a fun date," Tony said with mischievous grin.

"Look, Tony, I think you're nice. I'm enjoying this coffee, too. But if you keep asking me out, all you're going to end up doing is harassing me. Please don't do that. I've told you I'm involved with someone, and I need you to let it go, OK?"

"OK, OK. You can't blame a guy for trying. Don't be mad."

"I'm not angry; I just need you to stop."

"I will."

"Good." Serena glanced at her watch. "Whoops! I got to go. My cousin'll be here any minute. Thanks for the coffee." She slid off the bar stool and hurried out the door. Tony watched her retreating figure for a long time as he sipped the last of his coffee.

Serena hurried back to Cooper Hall and rushed up the stairs to her room. She got to

her door just as Troy was lifting his hand to
knock on it. "Good timing!" he said when he
saw her

"I'm psychic," she answered. The two
cousins hugged, and then Serena unlocked
her door. "C'mon in," she said. "I haven't
had time to clean, but the bed's made."

"You should see my room!"

Troy came in and dropped his overnight bag
on Serena's bed. He would sleep on an air
mattress on Serena and Tessa's floor this
weekend. For now, he flopped into Serena's
desk chair.

"So how are you?" Serena asked.

"I'm good. I'm just...well...swamped as
always."

Serena looked closely at her cousin. He
certainly didn't look good. Beneath his
cheerful attitude, she could tell he was under
some kind of strain. He looked as though he
hadn't slept much, and he seemed distracted.
"Is something wrong, Troy?" she asked.

"Why?"

"C'mon, Troy, it's me. You look awful!
Now tell me what's going on. Are you in
trouble at school or something?"

"No, it's not that. It's just ...well..." On the
spur of the moment, Troy decided to plunge
ahead. "OK, I owe some money, that's all,

and you know how my mom and dad are about that kind of thing."

"Well how much do you owe? Maybe I can lend it to you."

"It's not that much money, really, and it's no big deal. It's just annoying, that's all."

"Well, if it's not that much money, I can just lend it to you from my bank account."

"You don't have to do that."

"I don't mind. Really."

"You sure?"

"Yes, I'm sure." Serena fumbled in her purse for her checkbook. "Now, how much do you need?"

Troy stopped her with a hand. "Look, OK? I owe an awful lot of money. I just didn't want to make a big deal about it. It's more than you have in your bank account, though; I can tell you that right now."

Serena slowly put her checkbook back. "Troy, what is going on?"

Troy knew that if he told Serena everything, there was a good chance that his parents would find out. He couldn't risk that. On the other hand, he needed money desperately. He thought for a long moment and then said, "OK, I'll tell you. I was trying to be a nice guy, and I lent a friend some money so he could stay at Millworth. He never paid me back, and now I need to pay some bills and things. I can't tap my fund again until next semester, and I just know my mom and dad would kill me if they knew what I did, so I can't ask them for help. Dad's always yelling at me to be responsible. I'm pretty sure he won't consider that responsible."

"Why didn't you tell me in the first place?"

"I thought you'd think it was stupid."

"Well it is stupid, but it's good of you, too. So how much do you need?"

Troy mentally crossed his fingers. If this worked, he'd be all right. "I need twelve grand."

Serena paused for a moment. "OK, I don't have that much in my bank account, but I can get it from my trust fund. The bank's closed now, but it'll be open tomorrow morning. I'll get it then."

"Are you sure?"

"I think it was a really good thing for you to do to help a friend. Just consider it my way of helping, too.

"Thanks! And I swear I'll pay you back. I swear it! When I go home for Thanksgiving break, I'll go to my bank and tap my own fund and give it back to you."

"OK."

Troy reached over and hugged Serena. That had been a lot easier than he'd hoped, or had any right to expect. "So...you want to go get some dinner?"

"I thought you'd never ask. I'm starved."

"Where to?"

"Well, how about Tenderloins? They've got really good barbecue, and I love their salad bar."

"Lead on."

The two cousins rose, slipped their jackets on and left Serena's room. They decided to walk to Tenderloins, since it was only a few blocks from campus, and the evening wasn't very cold. Tenderloins was a brand-new restaurant that specialized in family-style service, steaks, ribs and sandwiches. The prices were reasonable and the atmosphere was relaxing. It was already becoming very popular with Tilton students.

When they got to the restaurant, Serena and Troy joined the line of Friday-night diners waiting for a table. After giving their names to the overly-cheerful greeter, they took seats on the long padded bench in the restaurant's lobby. After about fifteen minutes, they were whisked to a booth and handed menus, which both quickly opened and began to scan. In a moment or two, Serena said, "I don't even know why I'm looking at this menu. I already know what I want. I'm getting the ribs with mild sauce and going to the salad bar."

"Not me. That deluxe steak sandwich with mushroom gravy is more in my line."

Serena folded her menu and looked around to see if she could catch the eye of their server. Suddenly she looked down again and dropped her forehead into her hand.

"What's wrong?" Troy asked.

"Nothing really serious. It's just that there's this guy that's been pestering me to go out with him. I just saw him over there looking at me."

"Doesn't he know he's wasting his time?"

"I told him I'm seeing someone. He said he'd let it go, too. I just hope he's not here, well, watching me."

"Doesn't look like he is. He's got a friend with him."

"Still, it makes me feel sort of creepy."

"Well, don't worry. I'm here, too."

"Yeah, you are," Serena smiled, "and I'm glad of that."

At that, their server materialized and took their orders. By the time their food arrived and Serena had visited the salad bar, she'd almost forgotten her discomfort.

After dinner, Serena and Troy walked back to Cooper Hall. Serena wanted to get in an hour of practice before the eight o'clock floor meeting, so when they'd gotten to her room, she quickly pulled out her sheet music and violin, and rosined the bow.

"Hey," Troy said, "You mind if I go online while you're playing?"

"Not at all."

While Serena threw herself into her playing, Troy walked over to her desktop computer, turned it on, and was soon engrossed. Just before eight, Serena put her violin down, stretched her neck and arms and said, "OK, I need to go to my floor meeting. You going to be OK?"

"Oh, sure, I've got plenty to do. I brought some work along."

"OK, see you in an hour or so."

"Later."

Serena walked down the hall to the floor's large lounge area. It was decorated with utilitarian couches and chairs, a large beige area rug and a television. Tonight, one of the chairs had been dragged in front of the television, and Marcie Bratton was sitting in it, waiting for all of the floor residents to arrive. When the last straggler had shuffled in and taken a seat, Marcie began the meeting.

"OK, everyone. I've got just a few things for tonight, and then we can talk about what you guys want to do for our Finals Week Blowout. First, I found a couple of cigarette butts in the bathroom yesterday. You guys know you're not allowed to smoke in this building...."

After Marcie had made her announcements, the conversation turned to ideas for celebrating the end of the semester. After several residents had chimed in with their thoughts, Marcie drew the meeting to a close. "All right. I've written down everyone's ideas, and we'll vote on them at next week's meeting. See you all later."

In twos and threes, most of the other students rose from their seats and shuffled off to their rooms. A few remained in the lounge and, after Marcie had returned her chair to its normal place, turned on the television. When everyone had gotten settled, Marcie headed off to her room. She unlocked the door and said, "I'm back."

An answering, "About time" greeted her. Marcie shut the door behind her and then turned to face Lenore Hughes, an RA from Talmadge Hall, another dormitory on campus. Marcie reached out, smoothed Lenore's long, straight brown hair and said, "Stop complaining. I'm all yours now." The two girls embraced passionately as the faint sounds of the other residents echoed in the hall.

Chapter Three

"What can I do for you?" asked the accounts officer at Premier Pennsylvania Bank. The bank wasn't busy this Saturday morning, and Serena hadn't had to wait long for assistance.

"I'd like to make a withdrawal from my trust fund," Serena answered.

"Of course; we can take care of that for you. Let's go over to my office, and we'll get the paperwork done."

Serena followed the accounts officer to a small, semi-enclosed office area, where they sat down and began to discuss the withdrawal. As she filled out the required forms, Serena felt lucky to be able to help Troy. Years before, their grandfather had set up trust funds for each of them, to which each had gotten partial access starting at the age of eighteen. By the terms of that trust fund, Serena and Troy were allowed to withdraw funds only twice per year, and then only an amount equal to tuition and books fees at their respective schools. When they were twenty-one, the cousins would have full access to their money. Since Serena had a musical scholarship, she hadn't needed to use her trust fund this year, which was why she was able to help Troy. Serena's grandfather had originally intended his sons, Serena's and Troy's fathers, to administer the funds and to have access to the money. However, he'd quarreled with them over the running of the financial services company he'd inherited from his own father. The family conflict had gotten so serious that Serena's grandfather had fired his sons and rearranged the trust funds so that they would not have access to his fortune. Fortunately for both Serena and Troy, their fathers had good reputations in the financial services community, and were quickly able to recoup their lost money with other companies.

Now, Serena waited patiently while the accounts officer searched for her information on his computer. After a few moments, he looked up at her nervously and said, "I'm sorry, but I can't do this withdrawal."

"What? Why?"

"Well, I'm showing here that you've already withdrawn your allotment for this year."

"That's impossible! I haven't withdrawn any money from my fund at all this year!"

"Look, before you panic, let me look at this again, just to see what's going on."

"I'd appreciate that. I just hope nobody has hacked my account."

"I wouldn't think so. Our security procedures are strict. But I'll check for that, too. This might take a few minutes, though."

"I can wait."

Serena watched anxiously as the account officer examined her trust fund information. Like most other people, she'd heard horror stories of people who'd had their identities stolen. She did her best to be careful, but she knew that identity theft could happen to almost anyone. After a few seconds punctuated only by the sound of fingers clicking on a keyboard, the account officer looked up, red-faced. "I'm so sorry, Ms. Brinkman! I've made a terrible mistake."

"What do you mean?"

"Well, customer profile information is on a different page from the account information, for security. It turns out I accidentally called up another trust fund account with the same last name, but I didn't realize it was the wrong Brinkman until I looked up the profile. Your account is completely fine, and the funds are available for withdrawal."

"Can you tell me my balance?" Serena asked. "I want to make sure it's what I think it is."

"Yes, of course."

Serena took out her passbook while the account officer logged onto the correct account. After they'd compared notes (the amounts tallied exactly), the account officer said, "Now, let's take care of that withdrawal."

"Yes, thanks."

Within ten minutes, the transaction had been completed and Serena prepared to leave the bank. As she slipped her jacket on, she noticed the time displayed on her watch, and realized she'd have to hurry if she was to drop her things off at her dorm room and meet Troy and Patricia at the shuttle bus stop, as they'd agreed to do this morning. As soon as she left the bank, Serena half-ran back to Cooper Hall, paying nearly no attention to various people who called out greetings as she passed. She burst into her room, dropped her purse on her bed, and swiftly grabbed her backpack and the blanket she'd decided to bring. Stuffing the blanket into her backpack, along with her student ID and her cell phone, she glanced at her watch again, then zipped up the backpack, nearly slammed her door, and ran for the stairs, since the elevator would take too long. At last she arrived, breathless and just in time, at the shuttle bus stop where Patricia and Troy were waiting for her.

"What took you so long?" Patricia asked.

"The whole bank thing took longer than I thought," Serena answered.

"It went OK, though, right?" said Troy.

"Oh, yeah, no problem," said Serena.

"Good," Troy's look of relief was not lost on his cousin, who was somewhat surprised at how anxious he must have been. At that moment, though, the shuttle bus pulled up, and, as the students began to board, Serena put her trip to the bank out of her mind.

Serena wasn't the only one in a hurry that morning. Michelle Park's family would arrive on campus soon, and she wanted to be ready for them. Michelle wasn't planning to go to the Harvest Day activities; instead, her parents and younger brother would spend the weekend at Tilton. It didn't particularly bother Michelle to miss Harvest Day; she wanted to practice, anyway, and she had two papers to write. She'd rather have had the weekend to herself to get her work done, but she had learned the hard way not to go against her parents' wishes. It just wasn't worth the stress. Now, she hastily downed the last of her orange juice and left the cafeteria at a run. She'd arranged to meet her parents at her dorm room, and she didn't want them to have to wait.

Michelle was just in time. She'd barely opened her door and dropped her fleece jacket on the chair when she heard their voices coming down the hall. In a moment, they were at her door.

"I'm glad you're here," Michelle said as she greeted her parents and brother. "It's good to see you."

"How is your work going?" her father asked.

"I'm doing well this semester. So far, my grades are all As."

"Good. And your music?"

"The Young Artists' competition is on Wednesday. I think I'll be ready."

"You need to keep practicing, so you will be ready."

"I practice every day."

"Then you should be able to win."

"If you win, do I get to come with you on the tour?" This came from Michelle's brother, Daniel, who was two years younger than Michelle was.

"First, Michelle needs to win the competition," said their father. "Then we can talk about what you will do."

Michelle was glad when the conversation finally turned away from her accomplishments at school. She knew her parents cared about her, but most of the time, they only seemed interested in whether or not she was the best – the best at playing, the best in her classes, and the best at everything else. The pressure Michelle felt when they visited sometimes tempted her to make up an excuse not to see them. She knew, though, that putting them off would only delay the inevitable. She was just hoping she'd make it through the weekend.

By three o'clock that afternoon, the Harvest Day festivities were in full swing. Serena, Patricia and Troy had gotten to the university's farm at twelve, in time for the box lunches the university supplied. They'd all enjoyed the tour of the farm, although Patricia's fear of horses had meant she'd watched while Serena and Troy took rides around the paddock. After the tour, the three of them had decided to compete in some of the afternoon's events. Patricia and Serena had come in second in the three-legged race, and Troy had played on the winning team in the touch football game. Now, they were stretched out on the blankets they'd brought, watching the volleyball tournament.

"You should have gotten into the volleyball game, Patricia," Serena said. "You're a good player."

"No, thanks," Patricia murmured, half asleep. "I'd rather watch today."

"I know what you mean," Serena said.

All of a sudden, Troy nudged Serena, "Hey, Serena, there's that guy again."

"What guy?" Serena asked, half-turning her head.

"That guy that was at Tenderloins when we were there last night. The one you said keeps hitting on you."

"Oh, no!" Serena dropped her head onto her blanket. "I just hope he doesn't see me."

"Doesn't look like he's coming this way. He's just there."

"He kind of creeps me out," Serena said.

"Do you want me to say something to him?" Troy asked.

"No, please don't. I told him point-blank yesterday that I'm seeing someone and I'm not interested. I just hope he listens."

"Well, I wouldn't worry. Looks like he went away."

"Good."

"I'm going to go get a soda and see if any of the beautiful women here will have the good taste to notice me," Troy said jokingly.

"Anybody want anything?"

Both girls shook their heads. "No, thanks," Patricia said.

"Me, either," said Serena.

"Do you guys mind if I, well, look around for a while and maybe catch up with you in a bit?"

"No problem," Serena said.

"Thanks. How about if I meet you at the bonfire, OK?"

Patricia said, "Works for me. How about you?'

Serena nodded and said, "I'm good with that."

Troy got to his feet, stretched himself and said, "See you in little while, then." Then, he moved off towards the long tables that had been set up under some large oak trees.

Patricia, watching him leave, said, "Do you really think he's going to try to pick someone up?"

"He's better at it than you'd think."

"Serena, about that guy…"

"What guy?"

"That photographer guy. The one that's been following you."

"What about him?"

"I'd be careful if I were you."

Serena turned to Patricia. Something in Patricia's tone matched her own unconscious anxiety as she slowly said, "Yeah, I've been thinking about that, too. I mean, he hasn't threatened me, showed up at my dorm room, or anything way out of line. Maybe he'll back off."

"If he doesn't, you should talk to someone."

"Well, I will if I have to. He hasn't done anything yet, though. I mean, nothing threatening. Hopefully he won't."

"Well, just be careful. Does your RA know about him?"

"No, I haven't told her anything yet. You're right, thought, that's a good idea. Marcie ought to know about this. Maybe she can give me some ideas, too."

"There you go."

"OK, enough seriousness. This is supposed to be Harvest Day. Let's....harvest something."

"You're insane, you know that?"

Serena laughed, "That's what you love about me. Admit it!"

As the afternoon ended, everyone began to gather in the large, grassy field where the bonfire had just been lit. Serena and Patricia, who'd been wandering through the barn, made their way towards the growing crowd. Serena had used her cell phone to call Troy, so they could meet him for dinner. Patricia spotted him first and waved. Then she pulled on Serena's arm.

"There he is."

"Oh, I see him. Troy! Over here!"

In a moment, Troy had joined them.

"I see you're alone," Patricia joked. "No luck?"

"Not yet. The night is young, though," Troy retorted.

Serena said, "OK you two, let's get some food."

The three young people joined the long line of people waiting for skewers, hot dogs, corn on the cob and marshmallows. They found places near the bonfire and were soon roasting their hot dogs and corn. When the food was cooked, they spread their blankets on the ground not far from the bonfire and began to eat.

"Are you going to be OK with this food, Serena?" Patricia asked.

"It should be fine," Serena answered. Then, she explained to Troy, "Patricia tries to mother me. She's always worried that I'll accidentally get something with peanuts in it."

"Well, somebody has to."

"I know what I can eat and can't eat. Besides, I have you two mother hens to take care of me."

About twenty feet away, Tony Ferguson was eating dinner, too. It had been easy enough to find a place where he could watch Serena. There were enough people here that he could stay near her without being seen. She'd asked him to back off, and he would. For now. She probably just needed time. Tony hoped that that guy Serena was with wasn't her boyfriend. They didn't act like it, but she'd said she was involved with someone. Well, he could wait. Sooner or later he'd get his chance. He'd known since he met Serena that she was meant for him. Now he just had to convince her. As he finished the last of his hot dog, he tried hard to listen to what she was saying. Something about getting something with peanuts in it. Maybe she liked peanuts. He hadn't known that about her. He might be able to use that and get her a surprise. Wait; they were getting up and leaving.

Tony finished his soda in one gulp and followed Serena and the people she was with into the large barn, where a dance would begin soon. The animals had been temporarily moved to a smaller barn nearby, and the floor had been cleaned and covered with straw, except for a temporary dance floor that had been set up in the middle of the floor. The rest of the barn was decorated with small haystacks and pumpkins in strategic locations, and several long benches had been placed along the walls. Three long tables holding water, lemonade and various kinds of sodas were ready at the back of the barn. So were two tables full of cookies, candies and other sweet treats. The DJ was setting up, and some campus security police were getting ready to take their places. Tony found a place where he could watch the dancing and settled down. After a while, the music began and people started coming through the large barn doors in twos and threes. Before long, most of the seats on the long benches that lined the walls had been filled, and dancers were snaking to the floor. Tony watched as Serena and the girl she was with started to dance. He liked the way Serena danced; it was as graceful as her playing was. He noticed, too, that the guy they had been talking to had gone off to dance with someone else. Good. Maybe that meant that he wasn't Serena's boyfriend. For the next two hours, Tony watched Serena and the two people she was with as they danced, talked and laughed, and intermittently stopped to rest.

Patricia heaved herself onto the bench next to Troy. "OK, I am definitely going to work out more. This dancing is really taking it out of me!"

"You're having fun, though, I can tell," said Troy.

"Yeah, I am. I'm going to go take a break, though. I gotta go."

"We'll be here when you get back," Serena said.

"You'd better."

[67]

Serena and Troy watched as Patricia wended her way towards the ladies' room at the far end of the barn floor. After she'd gone, Troy said, "I'm going to have to leave early tomorrow and I don't want to wake you up. Did you put that check in my backpack?"

"Yeah, I did."

"Good. Thanks. And thanks for doing that. I hope they didn't give you a big hassle about it."

"Well, it was weird. I almost didn't get the money."

"What do you mean?"

"The accounts officer told me I'd already withdrawn my limit. When I said I hadn't, he looked again and said he'd gotten my account mixed up with another Brinkman."

"Didn't know our name was that common." Something in Troy's tone and expression made Serena look up. She'd known her cousin long enough to know when he was hiding something.

"Troy, I have to ask you something."

"OK, what?"

"Did you use your trust fund money to help your friend? Is that where you got the money?"

"OK, you caught me. I told you I didn't want my friend to get kicked out. So I gave him what he needed to tide him over."

"Which friend?"

"You wouldn't know him."

"Troy, come on. We've known each other all our lives and I know pretty nearly all of your friends. Who was it?"

"I told you, you don't know him. He's new this year."

"You don't give twelve thousand dollars to someone you just met. I keep thinking this over and something just doesn't make sense. What is going on? If you're in trouble, I want to know. I want to help if I can. But you have to tell me the truth."

Troy gulped. He had really wanted to avoid this conversation if he could. But Serena was too smart and too determined to give up that quickly. He wouldn't be able to keep brushing her off. Finally, he said, "OK, I'll tell you. I started to-"

"Hi, guys! I'm back," said Patricia.

Troy and Serena looked up, startled. "We didn't even hear you coming," said Troy, inwardly relieved to see her.

"Sorry if I scared you. You guys look so serious. Anything wrong?"

"No," said Serena. "Just cousin talk."

"Good. C'mon, Serena, this is a good song."

"OK." Serena turned to Troy and muttered, "We will finish this conversation," as Patricia took her arm. Troy nodded as the

[69]

two girls headed towards the dance floor. Saved again, but only for the moment, he would have to think of something fast.

By eleven o'clock, the shuttle buses had already begun to take the Harvest Day partiers back to the Tilton campus. Tony followed at a distance as Serena and her two companions got onto a waiting bus. He slipped in soon as he saw they weren't looking and took a seat at the back of the bus. After a twenty-minute ride, the bus stopped at Cooper Hall. It must be Serena's dorm, because she and her friends got up to leave. Tony followed them out and watched as they headed towards the building. Then he went into the building himself. He wasn't sure which floor Serena lived on, and he didn't want to risk them seeing him in the elevator. He was wondering what to do when he heard the girl with Serena say, "C'mon, we can handle the stairs. It's only the third floor!" She was voted down, and the three of them walked towards the elevator. Tony headed for the stairs.

Tony exited the stairs at the third floor and waited around the corner from the elevator until he heard the doors open and Serena and her friends get out. He heard one of them, the guy, say, "I'm heading to the bathroom. I'll be right there."

"OK," said Serena.

The two girls walked down the hall towards what must be Serena's room. Tony followed at a distance. He saw Serena pull her key out of her backpack and unlock her door. Then, he saw her say goodnight to her friend. Tony's face went pale and his green eyes widened as he saw the two girls kiss. What? Serena had a girlfriend? A girlfriend? This was too much for Tony to take. In confusion, embarrassment and anger, he turned back towards the stairs and, when he reached them, raced down them and out the side door of the building. Almost blindly, he rushed towards the off-campus dorm where he lived. He got to the building and ran up the two flights of stairs to his room. Right now, he was very glad he didn't have a roommate. He flung himself into his room and flopped onto his bed, his chest heaving. After a while, he started breathing more evenly and rolled over to face the wall, on which he'd tacked a picture of Serena. As he stared at the picture, his eyes begin to glitter with shame and anger.

Serena watched as Patricia walked down the hall towards the elevator. She'd had a good

time at Harvest Day, and was glad she'd
shared it with Patricia. Troy, too. She felt
lucky to have two people like them in her
life. She could count on them. Now, she
looked ruefully at her violin as she realized
she hadn't practiced at all that day. Well, it
was already eleven-thirty, and too late to
practice now. She'd get up early in the
morning and practice then. Troy interrupted
her thoughts as he came into the room.
"I'm back. Did you miss me?"
"Don't flatter yourself. Troy, I really think
we should talk about this whole money
thing. I know it's late, but I'm worried about
it. I really need to know what's going on."
"I told you before. I lent my allotment for
this semester to my friend so he could stay
at Millworth. What more is there to
explain?"
"I want to believe you. I really do. It's just
that somehow, it doesn't make sense. Are
you really telling me the truth?"
"Yes, OK? Stop worrying about me. As
soon as I pay my bills and things off, I'll be
fine."
"I guess so." Serena was still not sure Troy
was being completely honest with her. She
guessed, though, that the more she pressured
him, the less he'd say. She would have to
think of some way to get to the bottom of
what was going on. It wasn't so much that

she was afraid Troy was stealing from her;
she was afraid, though, that he was in some
kind of serious trouble that he wouldn't
admit. Maybe she should talk to his parents.
She was close enough to her uncle and aunt
that they wouldn't mind her asking. They'd
probably even be glad of her concern. She
would do that. She would ask them about it
at Thanksgiving break. For now, she gave
Troy a long look and said, "I hope you're
OK."

"I am."

At that point, the door opened, and Tessa
Oliver came in, tossing her backpack on her
bed as she did.

"Hey, guys! What's up?"

"Hiya, Tessa."

"Hey, Tessa."

Tessa unzipped her denim jacket and hung it
in her closet. Then she sat cross-legged on
her bed and asked, "Did you guys go to
Harvest Day?"

"We did," Serena answered, "But we didn't
see you. Were you there?"

"For a while. I went to dinner with my
physics lab partner, though, so we could go
over some things, so I didn't stay."

"You work too hard,"

"Look who's talking? You're always
practicing."

"That's different. That competition is going to be serious."

Tessa ran her fingers through her short, wiry black hair and said, "Stop freaking; you'll be fine. Marcie says you should be our floor's entry into the building talent show."

Marcie! All of a sudden, Serena remembered that she'd wanted to talk to Marcie about Tony Ferguson. She glanced at her clock; it was after midnight, but she knew Marcie'd be awake. Marcie frequently stayed up till two or three unless she had an early class. Serena said, "You just made me remember that I need to talk to Marcie about something. I'll be right back."

"You OK?" Tessa asked.

"Oh, yeah. I just have to ask her something. I'll be back in a sec."

Serena got up from her own bed and went down the hall to Marcie's room. She saw Marcie's light on under the door and looked at the sign in the shape of a clock that Marcie had posted outside her door. It had four labels: *Marcie Is Out*; *Come On In*; *Please Don't Disturb*; and *Be Right Back*. Right now, the arrow in the center of the clock pointed to *Come On In*, so Serena tapped on the door and pushed it open. "Marcie, do you have a second? I need to tell you about…"

Serena's voice trailed off as she looked into the room. Marcie was in bed with Lenore Hughes, one of the RAs from Patricia's dorm! Serena wasn't sure what to do, so she said, "I am so sorry, Marcie! Your door said, 'Come On In,' so I did. I didn't know..."

Lenore said, "It's OK, Serena. You didn't know."

"I'll – I'll just come back another time. It wasn't an emergency. Sorry!"

Serena backed out of the room as soon as she could and went back to her room. She'd had no idea about Marcie and Lenore, and she certainly hadn't wanted to walk in on anyone. That had been as embarrassing as anything she'd ever gone through, and her cheeks flushed as she thought about it. She took a breath and went into her room.

"Did you find Marcie?" asked Troy.

"Uh, yeah, I did."

"Good, let's get some sleep."

"Sounds good." Serena had no intention of telling anyone what she'd seen. You didn't tell the world about who was sleeping with whom, especially if that person was gay. Serena knew how she'd have felt if anyone had done that to her; she certainly would not do that to anyone else. She lay awake for a long while, though, thinking about whether she should say anything else to Marcie about it.

"Oh, my God!" Marcie said as soon as Serena had left her room. "What the hell am I going to do now?"

"Well, don't panic," Lenore said, trying to calm Marcie down.

"That's easy for you to say. You're not trying to have a military career. You don't just shout out to the world that you're gay if you want to be in the military. What if Serena tells someone? What if my C.O finds out?"

"Well, for one thing, Serena seems cool. I'm sure she won't tell anyone. Maybe you could talk to her. Explain what's going on and ask her to keep quiet. She didn't seem pissed or anything."

"Yeah, I guess I'll have to say something to her. I just hope to God she'll keep her mouth shut."

"For now, just try to get to sleep. You'll see her in the morning when you've both slept, and you'll talk to her then."

"You're probably right." Marcie didn't say anything more. She got out of bed, cracked her door open and changed the dial on her sign so that it pointed to *Please Don't Disturb*. Then, she went back into the room and lay back down on the bed. Soon, Lenore was asleep and breathing deeply. Marcie, though, lay awake for a long time, wondering how she would handle Serena Brinkman. She would have to do something quickly if she was going to save herself.

Chapter Four

At seven-thirty the next morning, Troy Brinkman looked over the contents of his backpack to be sure that he had everything. He looked twice to be sure that the check Serena had given him was zipped into the inside pocket. Once he was sure there was nothing he'd forgotten, Troy looked over at his sleeping cousin. He'd enjoyed the weekend, and was glad that Serena had been willing to help him out of his financial crisis. In a way, he wished he could have confided in her. The trouble was, though, that Serena would be too likely to tell his parents, and he couldn't risk that. Well, it didn't matter now; he had the money he needed, and he'd be able to take care of enough of his debt to stay out of court. He would just have to hope that Serena would let it go.

Thanks for everything! See you soon, Troy scribbled on a scrap of notepaper. He dropped the note on Serena's desk, took a last look around the room, and quietly left, easing the door shut behind him. As he headed towards the elevator, he saw Marcie Brennan, Serena's RA, walking towards him in the opposite direction.

"Hey, Marcie! You're up early," he said.

"Hi, Troy. I'm heading to the gym to work out."

"You have more discipline than I do."

"I don't know about that. Hey, is Serena up yet?"

"Not yet. Do you want me to wake her up?"

"Nah, I'll catch her later."

"If you say so. I've got to take off now. See ya."

"See ya."

Marcie watched uneasily as Troy pushed the elevator button and prepared to leave the floor. Had Serena told him what she'd seen? Did Troy know her secret? Would he tell other people? You never knew who would say what, and things got around, even on different college campuses. She was going to have to talk to Serena right away, before it was too late.

Resolved to make sure Serena would keep quiet, Marcie strode to her door. She almost knocked, but stopped short when she remembered that Tessa Oliver, Serena's roommate, was there, too. No need to involve more people in this; it would be better to wait until she could talk to Serena alone. Just then, the door opened, almost knocking Marcie over.

"I'm so sorry Marcie!! I didn't know you were there," gasped Tessa.

"It's OK," said Marcie, " Is Serena up yet?"
"She just woke up. Why? You want me to
get her?"
"No, thanks, I'll just stick my head in."
"OK, whatever." Tessa headed off towards
the large bathroom at the end of the hall.
After watching to see that Tessa had gotten
to the bathroom, Marcie tapped on Serena
and Tessa's door and stuck her head in.
"What's up, Marcie?" mumbled Serena in a
sleepy voice.
"Looks like you just woke up. You want me
to come back?"
"No, it's OK. What's up?"
"I need to talk to you about last night."

Serena propped herself up on her elbow,
then struggled to a sitting position. She'd
figured that she and Marcie would have to
talk about what had happened, but she
wasn't ready to do that before it was even
eight o'clock in the morning. Still, she
guessed that this was better than feeling
uncomfortable every time she saw Marcie.
She yawned widely, then said, "OK, but
Marcie, you don't have to explain anything.
Your business is your business. If you're
afraid I'm going to say something, don't be.
I'm not. I'm just sorry I walked in on you."
Marcie sat down on the end of Serena's bed.
"Look, Serena, I'm not sure you get it. The

military is not exactly warm and welcoming to gay people. They don't officially investigate people any more to see if they're gay, but you're not supposed to say anything about it or let anything get out. If word gets out to anyone on campus, I'm sunk. Dead. I will have no military career, and that's the only thing I've ever really wanted to do."

"I do get it, Marcie. I already told you that I won't say anything. I promise. Really. You think I want to jeopardize your future?"

"No, I don't think you want to. I just need to make sure that this stays between us."

"It will, OK?"

Marcie paused a moment. She didn't want to accuse Serena of betraying her, and she didn't want to seem paranoid. Still, she needed to be sure that she would be safe. Finally, she said, "OK. I believe you. Just please, please, don't say anything. Not to anyone."

"I won't, Marcie. Really."

Marcie smiled, patted Serena on the shoulder and said, "Thanks. And sorry if I woke you up."

"You didn't."

Marcie got up from Serena's bed. She said, "I gotta go work out. I'm glad we talked, though."

"Me, too. See you later."

"Yeah, later."

When Marcie had gone, Serena slowly got out of bed, stretched and shuffled to her closet where she pulled out a pair of jeans and a shirt. She wanted to get over to Lessner Hall and practice as soon as she could. Sunday afternoon was a busy time in the practice rooms, and she wanted to get there early. As she got her things together for her shower, she couldn't help feeling bad for Marcie. She herself couldn't imagine being that frightened for that long that someone would find out she was gay. She'd told her parents and Troy soon after she'd realized it herself, when she was a freshman in high school. At first, like the parents of many gay adolescents, her parents had been uncomfortable. Serena had been very lucky, though; her parents had put her happiness ahead of their own feelings, and they had come to terms with her homosexuality. Troy had accepted it, too, even more quickly; he had a few gay friends, so he hadn't been shocked. Serena knew how fortunate she was, and she had no desire to make Marcie's life difficult. She sincerely hoped that Marcie would relax and trust her to be quiet.

An hour later and a half later, Michelle Park and her family were just finishing breakfast at the Warm Welcome Inn, where Michelle's family had been staying while they visited her. The Warm Welcome Inn was a moderately-priced family-owned hotel that catered to visiting candidates for jobs and to the families of Tilton students. Its theme of rustic country hospitality was reflected in the breakfast menu, which featured hotcakes and sausage, country fried eggs, and biscuits with homemade gravy. As the family ate, Michelle's mother asked, "Do you need anything before we leave?"

"No, thanks," answered Michelle. "I think I have everything I need."

Michelle's father said, "What time is your competition on Wednesday?"

"The jury starts at one."

"Will there be a lot of competitors?"

"Only me and two other people."

"Who are these other people?"

"One is Ben Lessner. The other is Serena Brinkman."

"Are they good?"

"Ben won't be much competition. I swear the only reason he got picked is that his grandparents donated the money for the music building. He's not bad, but the jury probably won't pick him."

"Don't be certain of that. The jury may pick him. You will have to make sure that they don't. You will need to play your very best."

"I know that. You're just making me more nervous by saying it."

"Don't speak to me like that! I'm your father."

Michelle lowered her eyes contritely. "I didn't mean to be rude."

"Now, what about the other one?"

"Serena Brinkman? She's actually very good. She's here on a music scholarship, and she deserved it. If anyone can compete with me, it's Serena."

"So she has talent. You'll have to be even more careful about her. You will have to practice even harder and make sure that she doesn't win."

"I'm working as hard as I can."

"You have only three days until the competition. That means it's time to push yourself even harder. If you don't, one of those other people will win."

Michelle's mother interjected, "Please don't be so hard on Michelle. She's been working very hard and it'll be even more difficult for her if she's nervous and upset."

Michelle's father threw his wife a cold look and said, "Pressure is good for Michelle. She needs to keep working and practicing and not give up. If she doesn't feel pressured, she might stop working so hard."

"I don't think so. She wants to please us."

"We've talked about this enough. Michelle knows we have her best interests at heart. Michelle, do whatever you have to do to win that competition. We're counting in you to win."

"I understand. I will."

"Good. Now, since we're finished here, we should go back to our room and pack."

The family gathered everything together and left the dining room. Michelle followed her family up their room so that she could say goodbye. After taking her leave of everyone, and promising Daniel she would call him soon, Michelle picked up her violin, which she'd brought with her to the hotel, and walked slowly down the stairs from the family's hotel room to the lobby. She shrugged on the jacket she'd been carrying and zipped it up against the chilly morning air. It was a fifteen-minute walk from the hotel to campus, but Michelle didn't mind. She wanted to clear her head and do some practicing before her afternoon shift at FreshNow.

As Michelle walked, tears began to prick her eyes, and she blinked them back as best she could. The stress of being with her family had left her with a headache and indigestion, not to mention anxiety. Her parents had always been demanding, but in the past few years, it had only gotten worse. Now her father was expecting her to win the competition no matter what. That was almost too much pressure for Michelle to handle, even though she knew she had talent. Well, the only thing to do was just keep practicing. How was she supposed to do that and finish the two papers she needed to write, though? Her undone work making her feel even sicker, Michelle reached Lessner Hall and went immediately to the practice rooms in the basement. On the way to the practice room she usually used, Michelle passed other practice rooms which were already occupied by other musicians. She noticed that one of them was Serena Brinkman. As she heard Serena playing, all of Michelle's tension and anxiety seemed to come to the fore. If it weren't for Serena, Michelle would have no problem with the upcoming competition. That would get her parents to leave her alone and maybe even be proud of her. Ben Lessner wasn't a real rival, but Serena was very, very good.

Michelle forced herself to forget Serena for a while. She practiced her own piece until she had to get ready for work. She put her violin back in its case, picked up her case and jacket, and left the practice room. As she shut the door of the room, she turned and saw that Serena was leaving at the same time.

"Hi, Michelle," Serena smiled.

"Oh, hi, Serena," Michelle responded woodenly.

"I heard you playing. You sound good."

Michelle looked up in surprise. "Thanks, I think."

"I mean it. Just because we're competing doesn't mean I don't think you're good."

"Well...thanks. I have to go."

"Me, too. See you."

"Yeah, see you."

Serena turned and went towards the stairs that led to the building's lobby. She'd gotten halfway up the stairs when she realized she'd left her rosin in the practice room. She dashed back down the stairs and headed towards the practice room she'd been using. As she got close to the room, she stopped short. Michelle Park was slumped on the floor with her back propped against the wall, her knees drawn up and her head buried in her arms.

"Michelle, what's wrong," Serena called as she hurried to the other girl's side. "Are you sick or something?"

Michelle lifted her tear-stained face for a moment and murmured "It's nothing, OK?" Then she put her head back down.

"Come on, Michelle, something's wrong. I know we're not exactly friends, but if you're in trouble…."

"You wouldn't understand, Serena. I'm just under a lot of pressure. School, job, the competition – the whole thing."

"*I* wouldn't understand the pressure? I'm competing against the best violinist at Tilton, Michelle. Of *course* I understand the pressure."

Michelle looked up again. She hadn't thought of it that way. "Look, I'm just stressed, OK? I'll be all right."

"Listen, Michelle. How about we call a truce for a little while and I'll get you some of the best remedy there's ever been for stress."

"What are you talking about?"

"Come on. I'm going to take you to Sweet Dreams. My friend works there. They make the best ice cream sundae I've ever eaten."

"Well….."

"Come on, I could use a break, too."

"All right, I guess, but I have to work at two." Michelle said warily. She wasn't sure why Serena would be so friendly. After all, they were rivals, and Michelle's winning would mean Serena would lose. Still, Serena was possibly the only one who had a chance of understanding the incredible pressure that was brought to bear on anyone who wanted to win a musical performance competition. Almost unwillingly, Michelle straightened up, picked up her violin and slipped her jacket on.

"That's OK. I have stuff to do later, too," Serena smiled. "Just let me get my rosin. I forgot it."

Michelle waited while Serena ducked into the practice room she'd used and grabbed her rosin bag, tossing it into her violin case. When she'd closed the door behind her, the two girls went down the hall and up the staircase that led to the building's lobby and exit.

Located on one of Tilton's main streets, Sweet Dreams was a combination candy store and ice-cream parlor with a pink-and-white striped awning and an old-fashioned interior. All of the candy was made on the premises, so the aroma that wafted out the door when it was opened was irresistible. Serena and Michelle paused a moment to breathe in the sweet smell as they pushed the door open.

"I'm hungry already," said Serena.

"Me, too," Michelle admitted.

The two girls chose a small table near the counter and draped their jackets on the backs of two small ice cream chairs. Then, Serena boldly walked to the counter.

"Hey, does anybody *work* here? Or do I have to get served by a jerk - whoops – I mean 'soda jerk'?" she said to the girl behind the counter. At that, Michelle looked up in shock.

The other girl, dressed in a pink-and-white shirt, white pants and old-fashioned paper cap, said, "You're the jerk," and playfully tossed a paper napkin at Serena. Then the two of them burst into laughter.

Completely confused, Michelle said, "What's going on?"

"I'm sorry," Serena giggled, "This is my friend, Patricia Stanley. We've known each other for a long time. Patricia, this is Michelle Park. She's competing for first violin, too, and right now she's in desperate need of some ice-cream sundae therapy."

Patricia smiled, "Nice to meet you. Don't mind us, Michelle. We're both a little crazy. Now, what can I get you?"

"I'll have a 'Serena Special,'" said Serena.

"What's that?" Michelle asked.

"It's chocolate chip ice cream, banana pieces, and marshmallows mixed with pieces of fudge. Patricia tops it with whipped cream and a cherry for me. "

"Could I have one, too?"

"Sure! Two 'Serena Specials,' coming up," said Patricia.

Michelle watched as Patricia walked to the large stainless-steel freezer, opened the door and selected a small box of ice cream. She slipped on a pair of latex gloves and opened the container. Then, she opened a drawer beneath the counter and pulled out a clean scoop. She rinsed the scoop carefully, and then selected a clean dish, which she also rinsed carefully. Then, she put two scoops of ice cream in the dish. Next, she opened a cupboard behind the counter and pulled out a fresh bag of marshmallows and a packet of fudge. She opened each carefully and added fudge and marshmallows to the ice cream in the dish. After that, she peeled a banana and sliced it carefully, using the slices to decorate the dish. Finally, with a flourish, she sprayed the top with a generous dollop of whipped cream and placed maraschino cherry on the top. "One down, one to go," she said.

Serena waited to eat her sundae until Patricia had created another for Michelle. Then, the two girls sat down at the table and dipped their spoons into their treats. After the first bite, Michelle smiled, "This is heavenly! Thank you."

"What'd I tell you? Patricia makes an incredible sundae."

"She sure goes to a lot of effort. It must take her a long time if she has a lot of customers."

"Oh, that? That's because I have a really serious peanut allergy. Anything with peanuts in it could kill me. The only way I can eat anything in here is if whoever's serving me is really careful not to get anything with peanuts or peanut dust into my food. Patricia knows about my allergy, so I like to come in here when she's working."

"She's a good friend."

"Yeah, she is. Hey, Patricia! You have a new fan!"

"Thanks," Patricia looked up from the cash register where she'd been ringing up another customer. "I aim to please."

Serena turned her attention back to Michelle. "So what's going on? I mean, I know this competition is rough. It's killing me, too. Is that it?"

"That's part of it. I've got a lot of other things going on, too."

"I know what you mean. Tilton isn't exactly a party school."

"It's not, and my parents don't seem to realize how hard it is to practice all the time, do well in class, and compete, too. And I work part-time."

"Wow!! You must never sleep."

"It all just….gets to me."

"Can't say I blame you."

The two girls sat in silence for a moment or two, each remembering that she was talking with a rival. To cover their discomfort, they focused on their sundaes. After a short time, Michelle said, "I should really go. I have to be at work at two, and I have to go back to my room first and change my clothes."

"Actually, I should get back, too. I have an English paper calling my name."

Serena and Michelle spooned up the last of their sundaes. Then, Serena went to the cash register to pay while Michelle placed the empty dishes on the counter. After a few words with Patricia, Serena turned back to Michelle. "Ready?" she asked.

"If you are."

"I am."

The two girls waved to Patricia, who was taking another order, and left the store. As they left, Patricia looked up in time to see them walk out. What she saw next made her pick up her cell phone and call Serena. That photographer guy that had been following Serena was standing just across the street.

"So don't worry about it, OK?" Serena said into her phone. "He's not following me now, and I don't think he will. Besides, I'm not alone......yes, I'll be careful! See you later."

When she'd flipped her phone shut, Serena explained to Michelle, "That was Patricia – the one who just made those sundaes. She's paranoid because she thinks this guy that I know is stalking me. He's weird, but I don't think he's a stalker."

"I hope not."

Serena and Michelle walked the rest of the way back to campus in near silence. When they got to Cooper Hall, Serena said, "Here's my building."

"OK, I guess I'll see you tomorrow in class, then?"

"Yeah, guess so."

"Thanks for the ice cream."

"Yeah, sure."

Neither girl felt completely at ease with the other, but each had been glad of the other's company. With an awkward smile and wave, Serena followed the brick path that led from the street to the door of Cooper Hall.

Michelle watched her go, wondering what she was going to do about Serena. She didn't personally dislike the girl, and she was grateful for her kindness today. Still, there was no getting away from the fact that

Serena was a threat. Michelle was going to have to figure out what to do.

By three-thirty, Troy Brinkman had gotten back to the Millworth campus. He was actually looking forward to getting settled and starting the next week. The first thing he'd do would be to deposit the check Serena'd given him, and then call the finance company. At least they'd stop making his life hell. He was glad it had been so easy to solve this problem. He wasn't proud of himself for lying to Serena, but he didn't see that there was much choice. That extra two thousand that he'd asked for would let him make some real money online, too. With a sudden rush of gratitude towards his cousin, Troy decided to call and let Serena know he'd gotten back safely.

"Hey, Troy," Serena said.

"Hey. Just wanted to let you know I got here."

"Good. I'm glad you spent the weekend. I had a good time."

"Me, too."

"Troy, I've been thinking…. I think you need to talk to your parents when you go back for break."

"About what?"

"About this whole money thing."

"Serena, I told you!"

"No, listen. Something is going on. I don't know what it is, but I'm worried. I was willing to help you, and that's fine, but I think you need to let your parents know whatever it is that's going on. I think you're in trouble."

"I'm not in trouble, OK? Thanks for caring, but I'm fine. Like I told you, I'll pay you back if that's what you're worried about."

"It's not, and you know that. I'm worried about you."

"Well, you don't need to be, OK?"

"Just promise you'll talk to your parents, all right?"

"OK, I will."

"Good, I hope you do. I really think something's not right, Troy. I hate to put it like this, but if you don't talk to them, I will."

"OK, OK! I will."

Serena paused for a moment. "OK, look, I have to go. I'll see you soon."

"See you."

Troy tossed his phone angrily onto his bed. All of a sudden the sense of confidence that he'd felt about the future was gone. He had no doubt that Serena would make good on her threat to talk to his parents. He had to make sure that wouldn't happen. On the other hand, there was no way he was going to talk to them himself. Who knew what they might do if they found out about his gambling? At the very least, they'd do their best to cut off any access he had to any more money. They might even go further. There was no way he could risk Serena talking to his parents.

Serena closed her phone and put it on her desk. She truly hoped that Troy had meant what he'd said about talking to his parents. She didn't want to get herself in the middle of a family conflict, but the more she thought about it, the more she thought Troy might be in trouble. With a shake of her head, she went over to her closet and pulled out the full laundry basket that she'd neglected for longer than she should have. She tossed her cell phone, a small bottle of detergent and another of fabric softener on top of the load, and then fished in her top dresser drawer for her stash of quarters. After sliding six of them into her pocket, she patted her other pocket to be sure she had her room key. Then she shut the dresser drawer, picked up the novel she was reading for her English class and lifted the basket with a grunt. She headed down the hall and, when she got to the elevator, pushed the "down" button.

When the elevator arrived, Serena stepped in and went to the basement level, where laundry and kitchen areas were located. She thumped her basket down next to the first washer and opened the washer's lid.

"Hi, Serena."

Serena looked up and spun around, startled. "Tony, what are you doing here?" Tony Ferguson was standing just behind her.

"I want to talk to you."

"I'm sorry, but I'm starting to feel really weird about this. You know I'm seeing someone, but you keep following me around. I need you to leave me alone. Please. I don't want to make a big deal about this, but I will if I have to."

"I'm not here to scare you. I just want to talk."

"About what?"

"I saw you with that girl – the blonde. Is she – is she your girlfriend or something?"

"That's really none of your business."

"She is, isn't she? OK, fine, if you're seeing her, you are. Serena, all I'm asking for is a chance. I mean, you don't even really know me. I'll bet if we went out, you'd find out I'm a good guy. You might even change your mind about the kind of people you date. At least give it a try."

"Tony, you're not hearing me. I'm sorry to be so blunt, but please leave me alone. I appreciate that you profiled me for the *Vintage*, and I'm flattered that you want to go out with me, but I'm not interested. I'm involved with someone, and that needs to be the end of it."

"Serena…"

"I mean it, Tony. I don't think you're a bad person, and I don't want to call campus security on you or anything. But if you don't leave me alone, I will."

Just then, two other girls, both dorm residents, came down the hall towards the laundry area. Their voices relieved Serena more than she wanted to admit. When he heard the voices, Tony said, "OK, look. I don't want to hurt you. Like I said, I just wanted to talk. I'll leave now, but you'll see. You'll change your mind. When you do, I'll be waiting." With that, Tony shrugged on the windbreaker he'd been carrying and turned to leave. As soon as he was out of sight, Serena took a deep breath and leaned against the washer.

"You OK?" asked one of the girls.

"Uh, yeah, thanks. Just tired."

"OK," the girl shrugged. Then, she and her companion resumed their animated conversation.

As soon as she'd loaded her laundry into the washer, Serena called Patricia.

"Patricia, can you come over?" she begged as soon as Patricia answered.

"Why? What's wrong? You sound horrible."

"I'm a little scared. I think you might have been right about Tony Ferguson. He was just here and he really creeped me out."

"I'll be right there."

"OK, I'm in the laundry room."

"Got it. Be right there."

"Thanks! You're a lifesaver."

"That's what I'm here for."

While she waited for Patricia, Serena unsuccessfully tried to concentrate on her novel. When Patricia finally arrived, carrying two cups of coffee and a paper bag, Serena jumped off the washer where she'd been perched, and said, "I am *so* glad to see you!"

"It's OK. You'll be OK. But you know what? You really need to go to the campus police or something about this."

"What am I supposed to tell them? He hasn't hurt me or anything."

"You still should tell someone, hon."

"All right, I will."

"That's more like it. Now, let's eat and you can finish your laundry. Then I'll walk you over to the campus police. We'll tell Marcie, too."

"OK. What'd you bring? Besides the coffee, I mean."

"They made those waffle cookies you love at Sweet Dreams, so I brought some back."

"Thanks!"

As the two girls munched their cookies and sipped their coffee, Serena began to relax a bit. Patricia was right; she would talk to someone in the campus police, and she'd talk to Marcie, too. That conversation might be a little awkward, but she really should let her RA know what was going on, in case Tony was seen hanging around on the floor.

Chapter Five

Tony Ferguson rolled out of bed with a sleepy grunt. He'd stayed up most of the night finishing up a history paper that was due this morning, and had only dropped off to sleep two hours before. He'd intended to get it finished yesterday afternoon, since he usually set aside Sundays for working on longer assignments and projects. However, just when he'd settled down to work, he'd gotten a visit from the Tilton campus police. Tony still bristled with anger as he thought about that conversation. They'd actually suggested that he'd been stalking Serena Brinkman, and that he might risk expulsion if he didn't leave her alone. As if he would ever hurt her! All he'd done was talk to her. Now, he wasn't allowed in her dorm building, and the campus police had told him that they might advise Serena to file for a legal restraining order. They'd made it clear he was going to have to stay away from her. He couldn't even text her or call her – not even to talk about this whole stalking thing she'd made up. He felt a fresh rush of anger as he thought about the embarrassment Serena had caused him by reacting as though he were a common criminal. There was no way she was going to get away with that! As he began to think about having it out with Serena, Tony shuffled to his dresser and got his toothbrush, toothpaste, shaving kit and towel. Then he went out into the hall and towards the bathroom to get ready for class.

An hour later, Tony was walking across campus towards Jermyn Hall, which housed the History, Anthropology and Sociology departments. On his way, he passed near Cooper Hall, where Serena lived. He paused for a moment, and then turned towards the dorm. He wasn't sure exactly what he would do. He just knew he needed to straighten things out with her. All of a sudden he noticed a girl coming out of the building. He recognized her as the RA from Serena's floor and hurried over to her.

"Excuse me," he said. "Aren't you an RA in this dorm?"

"Yeah, I am. I'm Marcie Bratton."

"Is there a girl named Serena Brinkman on your floor?"

"Yeah, she – wait a minute! Who are you?"

"My name's Tony Ferguson."

"Look. I think you should know that Serena came and told me and the campus police about you. You need to leave her alone. You need to stay out of this building, too."

"I'm not going in the building. I just want you to give Serena a message for me."

"I'm not doing that. Leave her alone, and leave me alone, too. If you don't, I'm letting the cops know, and you'll get busted for felony stalking."

"Can't you just give her a message?"

"I said no. Now get out of here before I call the cops." Marcie held up her cell phone as a warning.

Tony paused for a moment. So this Marcie girl was in on it, too? She was protecting Serena, and getting in his way. There could be only one reason for that.

"Why are you hiding her? I'll bet I know why! You're jealous, aren't you? You like her! You're gay, just like she is! I'll bet the two of you are lovers. Did you know she's seeing someone else?"

"First, you're ranting and raving for no reason. Second, you still haven't gotten out of here."

"Just in case you didn't know, there's going to be an article in this week's campus newspaper about gays on campus. I'll bet you'll be featured in it!!"

"You have five seconds, starting now."

"Wait a minute."

"Four"

"OK, OK, I'm going. But I will straighten this out with Serena, whether you try to get in my way or not!"

With that, Tony stalked off. As Marcie watched him go, the color drained from her face. Although she had plenty of courage, Tony had shaken her up. No wonder Serena was worried about him. Marcie could just hope that Tony would take her threat to call the police seriously.

With two days to go before the competition, Serena had decided to spend as much time practicing as she possibly could. She'd even decided to take Dr. Montgomery's advice and practice with her Amati. That way, she'd be as comfortable playing it as she was playing her other violin. This morning, she'd been at Lessner Hall since eight o'clock, going over her piece and doing her best to polish up her work. Now it was nearly eleven, and time to stop if she was to be on time for her meeting with Dr. Berzin. She'd Emailed him asking if he would listen to her piece again before she played it for the jury. Today at eleven was the best time for him. Serena carefully placed her Amati in its case and closed it. Then she stretched her arms and neck and took a long drink from her water bottle. She picked up her violin and left the practice room. She decided to take the stairs up to Dr. Berzin's office instead of the elevator, since her legs felt almost as cramped from standing too long as her arms did from holding the violin.

As she walked up the stairs towards her mentor's office, Serena heard a voice behind her.

"Good morning, Serena. Are you ready for the competition?"

"Oh, hi, Dr. Montgomery. I think I am. Or at least, I will be."

"I'm sure you'll do a great job. I see you have your Amati with you today."

"Yeah, I thought I'd take your advice and practice with it, so I'll be comfortable playing it on Wednesday."

By this time, the two had reached the faculty offices on the second floor. Montgomery said, "Are you in a hurry, Serena? I wanted to ask you something."

"Well, I'm supposed to meet with Dr. Berzin at eleven, but I have a couple of minutes."

"Good. Come on in." Montgomery unlocked his office, shrugged off his lightweight trench coat and hung it on a hook attached to the back of the door. Then he circled behind his desk, sat down and waved Serena to the office's other chair.

"Serena, you know that I'm doing that paper on antique violins. I'd sure love to include your Amati in my work."

"You want to write about it?"

"Yes, I do. It's a wonderful specimen. The thing is that I'd need it for a day or so. I'd want to analyze its sound and really get a sense of it."

"I guess that'd be OK, but the competition is on Wednesday. Can I give it to you after that?"

"Yes, that'll be fine."

"All right. The competition is at two, so I can drop it off later on Wednesday."

"That would be great. Thanks!"

Realizing she was due to meet with her advisor, Serena said, "I'm sorry, but I need to go now. I have a meeting with Dr. Berzin."

"OK, and thanks, Serena."

Serena smiled and left Montgomery's office. She went next door to Sergei Berzin's office and tapped on the frame of his open door. Berzin looked up.

"Ah, so there you are, Serena. Come in."

"Thanks. And thank you for making time to hear me play."

"Of course. How else will I know if you are ready?"

Serena placed her violin case on the chair and opened it, taking out her sheet music, violin and bow.

"Now," said Berzin, "let me hear how passionately you can play."

While Serena was playing her piece for Sergei Berzin, Marcie Bratton was waiting for the members of her ROTC brigade to assemble. Now that she was in command of a brigade, she was determined to show her leadership skills. So far this semester, things had been going well. Her brigade was disciplined and was making progress in the field exercises and the other skills, like marksmanship, in which she led them. Today, the entire company would be working on drill and ceremony exercises. As the members of Marcie's brigade began to arrive, she took mental notes on their punctuality and appearance. Her observations were interrupted by a touch on her arm.

"Hey, Marcie, what's up?" This came from Kevin Gannon, a fellow brigade commander. They'd had several ROTC classes together, and had been in the same brigade when they'd entered Tilton.

"Not much, how are you doing?"

"Pretty good. Just trying to do too much. I might have to decide between doing ROTC and being a newspaper editor."

"I hope you don't have to do that."

"Me, too, but it's all taking up too much of my time."

"Oh, I have a question about the newspaper, actually." But Marcie would have to wait to ask her question. The company commander had signaled the start of drill.

Although Marcie's mind wasn't exactly on the drill, or on her brigade's conduct, she was good enough at leading the brigade that her team finished the exercises reasonably well. They'd need more work at formation and their timing could be a bit better, but overall, they'd done well. Marcie was glad of this, because she knew her company commander was carefully watching all of the brigade leaders. The better she looked, the more likely it would be that she could move up in rank. After she'd dismissed her brigade, Marcie went in search of Kevin. She caught up to him as he finished supervising his own brigade's dismissal.

"So what was your question about the paper, Marcie?" Kevin asked when he saw her.

"Do you know a photographer named Tony Ferguson?"

"Yeah, he does a lot of our photography. Why?"

"Well he was telling me about an article that's about to come out – an article about gays. Do you know anything about that?"

"Oh, yeah, it's going to be a whole thing about gays in leadership positions on campus. Bet you there are going to be a lot of ROTC people running scared about that article. You know how it is in ROTC."

"Yeah," Marcie said. "It's going to get ugly for some people. You know who's being interviewed for the article?"

"Well, I'm not the features editor, so I don't really know. I don't think the ROTC people lined up for it, though."

"Probably not."

"It's going to get very interesting."

"It sure is."

"Look, I gotta go. See ya."

"Later."

Marcie hurried off before Kevin started asking the obvious question of why she was so interested in the article. As she left, thoughts kept whirling through her mind. The newspaper article was going to include some interviews. One of them might be with Serena. She was already being interviewed for the *Vintage*, so it would be natural for the staff to think of her. If Serena was interviewed, she might very well mention Marcie's name. If that happened, Marcie would lose any chance she had of a military career, which she'd wanted ever since she was a child. Kevin hadn't mentioned Serena's name, but Marcie guessed that the author had to be Serena. She would have to get to Serena before she sent that article in.

Troy Brinkman read the Email from Serena with increasing panic. To tell the truth, he'd been worried about her ever since his visit to Tilton. Even though she'd bailed him out of his most immediate financial crisis, he knew that she was close to his parents. If she told them about the money, he would be in worse trouble than he'd been in before. There was no way that his parents would accept that story he'd told Serena about lending money to a friend. He hadn't even been entirely sure that Serena had accepted it. His fears had been confirmed when he opened her Email:

Hey, Troy

I've been thinking and thinking about this whole money thing. Like I said when you were here, I think you're in trouble or you wouldn't have needed that much money. I wish I could, but I just don't believe your story about lending money to a friend. Besides, when I was at the bank, the manager accidentally opened another Brinkman trust fund account when he was looking up mine. Troy, it had no money in it. If that's your account, and I think it is, you couldn't pay me back anyway, and you're in bigger trouble than I thought.

Whatever kind of trouble you're in, I think your parents need to know. I've thought a lot about this, and I think the only thing for me to do is tell your parents about it when we go home for Thanksgiving break. Maybe even sooner. I don't want to do it behind your back, though, so I'm letting you know now. I'm sorry if this upsets you, but I think you're in over your head and I want to help. Hope we talk soon –

Serena

Now Troy had no idea what he was going to do. He was going to have to find some way to stop Serena from talking to his parents, or even to her own. Troy didn't want to take more time away from his classes, but there was no way around it. He was going to have to go back to Tilton and deal with Serena. He thought of Emailing her that he was coming, but decided against it. He didn't want to let her know how seriously worried he was. Instead, he thanked her for caring and said they'd talk about it soon. That message sent, Troy closed his Email and started planning an impromptu trip to Tilton.

He had classes the next day, but he'd go on Wednesday. Serena was competing on that day and it would be a good excuse to visit without seeming too anxious.

Not to worry, Serena, the note said. Well, it was like Troy not to take life seriously, Serena thought. She'd returned to Cooper Hall to drop off her Amati after her practice session and lunch, and was now catching up on her Email. Troy's Email said that they would talk about the money she'd lent him next time they saw each other, but who knew when that would be? Troy knew about her competition on Wednesday, but he'd already said he wasn't sure he could make it. Serena decided that she would definitely have to talk to his parents. Whatever was going on in Troy's life, it was serious, but he wasn't dealing with it. Serena knew that Troy didn't always get along with his parents, but he needed someone to set him straight, and he obviously wasn't listening to her. With an irritated sigh, she decided she'd call Troy at some point, and then moved on to the other messages waiting for her.

Her reading was interrupted by a knock on her door.
"Come on in, it's open," she called.

Serena's door opened and Marcie Bratton came in. "I need to talk to you."

"What's wrong?" Serena asked.

"It's about that interview you're doing for the newspaper."

"What interview? What are you talking about?"

"Don't play dumb. I heard from one of the editors that they're doing an article about gay people in leadership positions here on campus. You're going to be interviewed, and you're going to mention me, aren't you?"

"I'm not being interviewed for any article. I barely have time for my schoolwork with the competition in two days."

"I don't think you get it, Serena. Nobody can find out about me. Nobody. If anything gets out, I'll have to get out of ROTC, and I'll have no chance at all at being an officer. You can't say anything about me."

"I told you, Marcie, I'm not getting interviewed for any newspaper article. I'm sorry someone gave you the wrong idea, but I'm not. Really."

Marcie looked for a long moment at Serena. Then, slowly, she said, "You can't say anything about me, Serena. Not to anyone. Not even to Patricia."

"I haven't, OK? And I won't. Will you stop worrying?"

"I hope you won't." With that, Marcie left Serena's room.

As she walked down the hall towards her own room, Marcie thought about how dangerous Serena could be to her. Even if Serena wasn't writing that article (there were, after all, plenty of other people living in Cooper Hall), she was the only person who knew Marcie's secret. Tony Ferguson didn't count; since he'd been stupid enough to bother Serena, he was regarded as a loose cannon whom nobody would believe. But Serena was different. Marcie began to realize that the only way to safeguard herself and her career would be to ensure that Serena kept her mouth shut.

Marcie had only been gone for a few moments when Tessa came in.
"Oh, good, you're here."
"Why? What's up?"
"I just saw Patricia coming up in the elevator. She's in the bathroom and then she's on her way here."
"Oh, thanks."
"So," Tessa gestured towards Serena's violin, "Are you ready for Wednesday?"
"I think so. So does Dr. Berzin. He listened to me again today, and he didn't have that

many criticisms. Hopefully, I'll have a few hours to practice later on today."

"Well, don't let me stop you. I like it when you play."

"If you insist," Serena said with a smile. She pulled her violin out of its case and was soon so intent on her playing that she didn't notice when Patricia came into the room. When Serena finished her piece, Patricia applauded, startling Serena.

"You scared the hell out of me! I didn't even know you were there!" Serena gasped.

"Sorry. I just didn't want to disturb you. You are really sounding ready for that competition."

"Thanks. You're going to be there, aren't you?"

"Wouldn't miss it."

"Thanks. That means a lot."

Across campus at Lessner Hall, Michelle Park drew her bow across her violin strings in the last measure of her competition piece. Then she looked up hopefully at Sergei Berzin.

"What do you think?" she asked.

"Michelle, you have tremendous talent, and you have chosen a fine piece."

"Am I ready for the competition?"

"Technically, yes. You know the piece very well and you play it professionally. You will need to keep practicing so that your love of the piece is also obvious."

Michelle thanked her advisor and returned her violin to its case. She was tempted to ask Berzin whether he thought she could beat Serena Brinkman, whom she knew was also Berzin's advisee. She thought better of it, though, as she knew that Berzin was far too professional to reveal any preference he had for one or the other of his star performance students.

For Berzin's part, he was proud to mentor both girls. Talent like Michelle's and Serena's might come along a few times in a faculty member's career, but to have two such gifted students at once was truly remarkable. Since the girls were rivals, one might have expected jealousy, even mean-spiritedness. However, neither girl had stooped that low. Each had treated the other with respect, and that had made his job much easier. For that he was also grateful. Now, he dismissed Michelle with a smile and a piece of advice. "Focus on your own playing, and try to forget the other competitors. You will do better that way."

"I will. Thank you."

Michelle left Berzin's office and slowly went down the stairs to the ground floor of the music building. She thought again and again of Berzin's comments, trying to get whatever clues she could from what he'd said. Berzin himself would not be on the jury Wednesday, but he was honest enough to tell her the truth about her playing, and he was experienced enough that he would know what the jury would expect. As she left the building, Michelle grew more and more concerned. Berzin hadn't said that she could win. He hadn't even really said she was ready for the competition, except that she knew the piece well. What did that mean? Did that mean that he thought Serena was better? Or had he spoken that way to make sure Michelle kept practicing? Maybe he thought her playing wasn't passionate enough. Maybe he thought Serena would win, and didn't want to tell Michelle for fear she wouldn't do her best.

By this time, Michelle had returned to her dormitory building, Gladstone Hall, and gotten up the two flights of stairs to her floor. She unlocked her door and absently placed her violin on her bed and pulled off her jacket. Then she sat on her bed next to her violin and stared out of her window, trying to focus her thoughts. Michelle couldn't afford to lose this competition. It was difficult enough to stay in her parents' good graces. If she lost the competition, she would likely also lose her life at Tilton. That would be too much for Michelle to handle. On the other hand, she didn't personally dislike Serena, and didn't wish her harm. If only Berzin had given her some clue as to what she would need to do to beat Serena. After a while, her scattered thoughts began to settle themselves. She must win this competition; there was no other option. So she would need to make sure that Serena didn't.

At nine-thirty that evening, Serena and Tessa were stretched out on their beds. Serena was finishing the second of three novels she'd been assigned to read for her English class. Tessa was preparing for an exam in Linear Algebra. They'd found that studying together wasn't a problem, as they both preferred to work without TV or music, and with a minimum of conversation. As they worked, each girl occasionally stretched out a hand towards the snacks that lay on the beds beside them. Tonight, Tessa was eating potato chips, while Serena had a bag of fresh popcorn. After about an hour,

Serena lazily tossed a piece of popcorn at Tessa to get her attention.

"Hey, Tessa, you ready for a soda break?"

"OK."

The roommates got up and got some change. They went down to the ground floor of the building, where there was a combination game room/lounge that included three vending machines. After the girls had gotten their drinks, Tessa said, "You want to play some pool for a bit? I'll kick your butt."

"Don't be so sure of that. But only one game, OK? I really have to get that novel read."

"One game is all I'll need to beat you," Tessa joked. The girls racked up and began to play.

When the game, which Tessa won, was over, the girls prepared to go back to their room. As they crossed the lobby of the ground floor, Serena saw Michelle Park standing uncertainly at the elevator.

Michelle turned at the sound of Serena's and Tessa's approach. "Serena! I'm so lucky it's you. I thought you lived in this building, and I really need to talk to you."

Serena was caught completely off guard. "OK," she finally responded. Then she turned to her roommate. "You go on up. I'll be up in a minute."

"OK, see you upstairs, then."

After Tessa had left, Serena gestured
towards a large couch on the other side of
the lobby and said, "Let's go over there."
Michelle nodded and they were soon seated.
"So what's going on? What's wrong?"
Serena asked.
"This competition coming up on Wednesday
– it's really important to me. It means just
everything."
"It means a lot to me, too. I'm really hoping
for concertmistress."
"Serena, you don't understand. Even if you
lose the competition, you'll have other
chances at concertmistress. You'll get
noticed. You'll have a career. If I lose, it's
the end for me."
"What do you mean?"
"I'll probably have to drop out of Tilton if I
lose."
"Drop out? Why? You're incredibly
talented."
"It's my parents. They simply won't accept
it if I lose. I have to win. I just have no
choice if I want to keep playing."
"So what are you saying? Are you asking
me to drop out of the competition?"
"I can't ask you to do that. I just want you to
know how important this is to me. You can

win other competitions. I won't be able to if I lose this one. I'm just asking you to think about that when you play on Wednesday."

"You're asking me to play less than my best? Michelle, you know how good you are. You don't need any favors from me to win. If you win, it'll be because you're better. Besides, this competition is a big deal for me, too. It's really important. I'm not concertmistress here at Tilton, and now I have a real chance at it. Why would I give that up?"

"I know it's important to you, and I'm sorry. But I have a lot more at stake. You don't get it, Serena. I have to win."

"I'm sorry you're under so much stress, Michelle. I really am. But I can't do what I think you're asking me to do."

"All I'm asking you to do is think about the other chances you'll have and have a little compassion, OK? Look, I have to go. Just please, think about it."

Before Serena had a chance to respond, Michelle had risen from her seat and headed towards the door of the building. As she watched the other girl leave, Serena felt conflicted. She was sympathetic towards Michelle. Pressure from parents could be unbearable, and Serena was well aware that she was lucky to have supportive parents. On the other hand, Serena had dreamed of a performance career for almost as long as she could remember. She had no desire to derail her own career plans to do a favor for a rival. In this distracted state of mind, she turned towards the elevator and, when it arrived, returned to her room where Tessa had returned to her studying.

Chapter Six

Serena woke with a start on Wednesday morning. She glanced at the digital clock by her bed – four o'clock! It was too early to get up, but she didn't feel at all like sleeping. For a while, she tried to find a more comfortable position to try to go back to sleep, but after about fifteen minutes, she gave up and quietly slipped out of bed. Grabbing her chemistry book, she padded towards the door. Once or twice she glanced over at Tessa's sleeping form. Serena had no wish to waken her roommate. At the door, she paused to make sure she had her cell phone and room key, then left the room and went down to the lounge. Hopefully if she tried to study for a while, she'd feel sleepy enough to go back to bed.

"Just nerves," Serena thought to herself as she settled in the lounge. She wasn't really surprised at not being able to sleep. The competition was at two o'clock, and, although she'd practiced for several hours yesterday, she could still point to places in her piece that needed work. Or maybe she was just being too hard on herself. Maybe she was ready. Serena grew steadily more irritated with herself for being so anxious. She'd practiced as much as she could, and she knew that the more confident she felt, the better she would play. With a shake of her head, she opened her chemistry book and tried to focus on polymers.

At seven, Tessa awoke and noticed that Serena wasn't there. After a moment, her head cleared and she remembered that Serena's competition would be today. No wonder she was gone. She'd probably gone over to Lessner Hall to practice. Tessa quickly gathered her shower things and towel; she wanted to have enough time to clean up and stop for coffee before her eight o'clock class.

At eight-thirty, Marcie Bratton left the bathroom where she'd just finished her own shower. Instead of going directly to her room, she went to the lounge to check the weather forecast on television. There, she saw Serena lying fast asleep on one of the sofas. Marcie went over and touched Serena gently on the shoulder. "Hey, wake up," she said.
Serena's eyes flicked open. Then, realizing where she was, she sat up quickly. "I must have fallen asleep studying," she said.
Marcie glanced at the book lying on the floor next to the sofa. "Chemistry'll do that

to you," she said. "Now come on, Sleeping Beauty. Time to get up and get going."

"Right. Thanks," Serena said as she struggled to her feet.

"Your competition is today, isn't it?"

"Yeah, it's at two."

"I wish I could be there, but I have class. I know you'll win, though."

"Thanks."

"Hey, you want some breakfast or some coffee or something?"

"No, not yet. Right now I need a shower. Maybe later."

"OK, well let me know when. It's on me."

"OK, that'd be great."

As Marcie returned to her room, Serena rubbed her eyes and collected her thoughts. It was nice of Marcie to offer to buy breakfast, and Serena hoped that meant that Marcie no longer worried about her privacy being violated. In the meantime, Serena had plenty of other things to think about, most notably that it was quarter to nine and she had a ten o'clock class. She rushed back to her room, tossed her book on her bed and hurriedly gathered her shower kit.

By nine-forty, Serena was dressed and ready for class. As she was filling her backpack, she heard a tap on her door.

"C'mon in," she called.

Marcie entered, holding a large cup of coffee and a bagel. "Here," she said. "I know you have to get to class, but at least take this with you."

"Thanks a lot!" Serena said. "I need a jolt."

"And it's supposed to be chilly today, so you'll want your jacket."

"Thanks."

She took the coffee from Marcie's outstretched hand, tossed the bagel in her backpack, picked up her violin and jacket and hurried off to class. She arrived at Lessner Hall and her History of Music II class with only moments to spare, and slid into a seat. Pulling her notebook out of her backpack, she opened it to a blank page, fished a pen out of the front pouch of the backpack, and prepared to take notes. As class began, Serena took a long drink of the coffee, thinking again how nice Marcie had been to give it to her.

At eleven o'clock, when class was over, Serena went down to the building's basement for some practice time. Thankfully, few of the practice rooms were occupied, so she was able to quickly settle into her favorite room and begin her piece. She ran through it twice, stopping here and there to replay measures that she felt needed improvement. When she was satisfied, she played the entire piece once more. Finally, she packed up her violin and rosin and prepared to leave. It was nearly noon, and although she wasn't hungry, she decided it would be a good idea to eat at least something. She thought for a moment about the bagel Marcie had given her, but she wasn't sure where Marcie had gotten it, so she couldn't be sure it wouldn't be cross-contaminated with peanuts somehow. Sometimes having to be very careful about what she ate could be really inconvenient. Serena was just about to leave the building when she heard her name being called. She turned around to see Troy running to meet her.

"Troy, what are you doing here? You didn't tell me you were coming. I meant to call you, too, about your Email."

"We can talk about that later. Right now it's your moment. I wouldn't miss your big day. I figured you'd be here practicing, so I decided to come straight over."

"Well, thanks. Where are you staying? Are you spending the night?"

"No, I'm just here for your performance. And to take you to lunch if you want."

"That'd be great. I'm not hungry, but I was just thinking I should eat something."

"You really should."

"Let's just go to the Pit Stop. They have snacks and sandwiches."

"OK, lead on."

The two young people crossed the grassy mall that lay between Lessner Hall and the Student Union building. As they walked, they tossed up the hoods of their jackets against the chilly wind that had sprung up. At the Student Union building, they put their hoods down, unzipped their jackets and headed towards the Pit Stop. When their turn came to be served, Troy picked up a roast beef sandwich and a bottle of soda, and Serena chose a salad package and an orange juice. For a moment, she studied the label on the salad package to be sure it was safe. Then, she hastily moved to catch up to Troy, who was already at the cash register. When they'd paid, they took seats at one of the few small tables. Serena had just taken the lid off her salad packet and opened her orange juice when she said, "Troy, can you watch my backpack for a minute? I need to go to the ladies' room."

"Sure, no problem."

When Serena returned from the ladies' room, she thanked Troy, sat down and began to eat. After a bite or two, she said, "I'm really glad you're here today. Mom and Dad can't make it, so it'll be nice to have family in the audience."

"Is Patricia going to be there?"

"Oh, yeah. In fact, she's going to video the whole thing so I can put it on my blog and send it to everyone."

"That's great."

"Look, Troy, I'm actually glad you're here anyway. We need to talk about this whole money thing. I meant what I said about talking to your parents."

"You don't need to do that, Serena. I've been thinking about it and maybe you're right. I should probably tell them."

"You mean that?"

"Of course I mean it."

"I'm glad to hear you say that. It was either you tell them or I tell them and I think it's better if you do it."

"Like I said in my note, not to worry. Everything's going to be taken care of."

"If you say so."

Serena was preoccupied enough with the competition that she decided to drop the subject for the moment. She made a mental note, though, to follow up and see if Troy actually would talk to his parents.

When Troy and Serena had finished eating, Serena said, "I need to go back to my room

and change and then get ready for the competition. Will you be OK on your own?"
"Sure. I'll check out the campus a bit and then go over to the music building."
"All right. See you later, then."
"Not if I see you first," Troy joked. Serena tossed her napkin at him, laughed, and then picked up her trash and threw it into a nearby trash can. She gathered her things, waved to Troy, called, "See you," and then left The Pit Stop.

Serena hurried back to her room, stopping on the way to take her Amati out of the dorm safe. Fortunately, Tessa wasn't there. Normally, she enjoyed Tessa's company, but right now, she was far too nervous to want to make conversation. She needed to focus herself and get ready to play. She carefully changed her clothes, putting on the black top and skirt that she wore for competitions. Then she combed out her hair, touched up her makeup and took a long look at herself in the mirror that hung above her dresser. Satisfied with what she saw there, she took her auto-injector of epinephrine out of the jeans she had been wearing and put it in the accessory pocket of her violin case. After she'd closed up the violin case, she took one last glance in the mirror,

[131]

straightened her shoulders, picked up the Amati and went over to Lessner Hall, where she knew the jury was already gathering.

Backstage at Lessner Hall's auditorium, Michelle Park sat next to Serena while they waited to perform. Right now, Ben Lessner was just finishing up. The girls said little as they opened their violin cases, rosined their bows and prepared to play. After a few moments, they heard the applause that signified that Lessner was done. Within seconds, Lessner passed them as he exited, saying, "Good luck, you two. That jury looks tough!"

"I'm sure you did well," Michelle said in reply. Serena nodded her agreement.

In a moment, one of the stagehands came towards them saying, "OK, Serena Brinkman. You're up."

With that, Serena rose, picked up her violin and bow, and said, "Well, here goes."

Michelle looked up at her with almost pleading eyes and said, "Please remember what I said."

Serena said, "I haven't forgotten," and walked onstage.

In a moment, she had taken a bow and begun to play. Michelle's heart sank as she listened. Serena was playing brilliantly, better than Michelle had ever heard her play before. Every note was perfect, and Serena had caught all of the nuances of the piece. There was no doubt about it; the jury would love her. Tears began to fill Michelle's eyes as she contemplated what this would mean for her. Serena couldn't win! She just couldn't take away Michelle's only chance.

As Serena finished her piece, she glanced out at the faces of the jury. She was pleased with what she saw there; they were smiling and nodding, and it was clear she'd done well. Then she looked at some of the other people in the audience. There was Patricia, beaming at her from the second row. Next to her was Sergei Berzin, who looked as proud as Serena had ever seen him. Troy was on the other side of the auditorium. He must have slipped in late. Serena was really glad that people she cared about were there to support her. She took a bow and went backstage where Michelle and Ben were waiting.

"You did great!" Ben said. "Lots better than I did." Serena smiled her thanks.

Michelle gave her a thin smile but said nothing as she picked up her violin and bow and went on stage for her own performance.

While Michelle was playing, Serena sat next to Ben and took a few deep breaths. Now that her performance was over, she was hoping she'd be able to relax a bit. Whatever happened now, she knew she'd done her best. After a moment, she started to focus in on Michelle's performance. She was doing very well. Serena knew that if she didn't win the competition, it would be because of Michelle's skill. Serena would have liked to see how the jury and audience were reacting, but from her angle, she couldn't see them. No matter; soon enough they would all be called back onstage to hear the jury's decision. When Michelle finished her piece, Serena heard the audience applauding. It was well-deserved, too. Michelle had played very, very well. A moment later, Michelle returned to the backstage area, gulped and sat down.

"You played really well," Serena said. "You could win this."

Michelle gave her a long look. "You played well, too," she responded.

Almost before they knew it, a stagehand was beckoning the three violinists. One after another, they filed onto the stage and took a bow. They waited for silence, and then the jury foreperson spoke.

"All three of you deserve congratulations. You all played very well, and you all have excellent prospects for music careers. That made the jury's decision particularly difficult. However, there can be only one concertmaster or concertmistress. This jury has selected Serena Brinkman as concertmistress for the Young Artists' Orchestra. Congratulations, Ms. Brinkman, on an outstanding performance."

Michelle stared dully as the audience, including the jury, rose to applaud Serena. There was Ben, hugging Serena, and a stag hand passing her a bouquet of roses. Now it was Michelle's turn to congratulate her rival. Like an automaton, she gave Serena a quick hug and joined in the applause. What else could she do at this moment? When the applause began to die down, and the cameras had stopped flashing, the three violinists left the stage. They stopped backstage to pick up their violin cases. When they got there, Serena said, "You guys go on. I have to sit for a second."
"You OK?" Ben asked.
"Yeah, just a little stomach acid from nerves."
Michelle said, "I have some antacid if you want some."
"That'd be great. Thanks."
Michelle reached into her bag and pulled out a package of chewable antacids. She pulled

one out of the package and handed it to Serena, who said, "Thanks."

Serena unwrapped the antacid and popped it into her mouth. Then she walked over to a nearby trashcan and tossed the wrapper into the trash, brushing the antacid's nonstick powder from her hands as she did so.

The three performers left the backstage area. Michelle and Ben headed to the lobby, where there was a reception for all of the orchestra's competitors. Serena headed in the opposite direction, and Ben called, "Aren't you coming to the reception?"

"I am. I just have to run upstairs for a moment first. I promised Dr. Montgomery I'd lend him my Amati for a paper he's writing, and I want to drop it off."

"OK, see you there."

Serena waved in acknowledgement and turned to go upstairs towards Jesse Montgomery's office. When she got there, she saw that his door was open, so she tapped on the frame.

"Oh, Serena! Come on in. Congratulations! Dr. Berzin just told me you won the competition."

"Thank you. I'm really happy about it."

"Well, you deserve the win. You play superbly."

"Thanks. I wanted to stop up and drop this off before I forget."

"How nice of you to remember! I will thoroughly enjoy including your Amati in my paper. If I may have it for the rest of the week, I can give it to you on Monday."

"That'll work."

Montgomery gently took the violin from Serena and carefully laid it on his desk. He opened the case and tenderly took the Amati from its resting spot. His eyes glowed for a moment as he looked at the violin. He placed it back into the case, closed it, and promised, "I'll take good care of this. Now, let's go down to the reception. I promised to bring a bottle of champagne for it."

Montgomery opened the bottom of his two desk drawers, pulling out a bottle of champagne. He shut the drawer and the two of them left his office. They stopped briefly at the Music Department's main office where Montgomery locked the Amati in the department's safe. When they got down to the lobby, they could hear the loud hum of voices as performers and members of the audience mingled at the reception. Montgomery said, "Why don't you go and celebrate. I'll bring you a glass of champagne."

"OK."

When Serena joined the group, she was soon surrounded by a group of people congratulating her. As she thanked them, Montgomery elbowed his way towards her, proffering a glass of champagne. Serena thanked him and took a long sip. This was really happening! She was to be concertmistress! For the first time in weeks, she began to relax a bit.

An hour later, Serena and Patricia left Lessner Hall. As the two of them walked towards Cooper Hall, Patricia said, "So, Ms. Concertmistress, you want to go out tonight and celebrate?"

"Maybe. Right now I'm so tired I can't even think straight. I can't wait to get back to my room, lie down and take a long nap. I'm so glad I don't have any classes the rest of the day."

"OK, well, you want me to call you later?"

"That'd be great. Call me around five-thirty, OK? We'll go somewhere and eat."

"Got it."

By now, the girls had reached Cooper Hall. Patricia gave Serena a quick hug, said, "Night night," and turned to go to her own dorm building. Serena went into her building and, after checking her mailbox, went upstairs, flipping through her mail as she went. As she got out of the elevator, she saw Marcie walking down the hall towards her from the bathroom. Marcie called out, "Hi, Serena! How'd it go?"

"I won!"

"Oh, that's great!!" Marcie came up to Serena and gave her a hug. Then, she said, "You don't look so good. Are you OK?"

"I think I'm just wiped from the competition. When you perform, your adrenalin just goes crazy, and after it's over, you crash."

"I can understand that. Well, nobody's around now, so you should have some peace and quiet for a nap."

"Good! That's just what I plan to do."

"Sweet dreams, then," Marcie smiled. Serena thanked her and went into her room and tossed the mail on her desk. She quickly changed her clothes, carefully hanging up her outfit and putting on sweat pants and a t-shirt. She flopped onto her bed and was soon fast asleep.

An hour later, Serena awoke, gasping for breath. It wasn't exhaustion! Immediately recognizing the signs of anaphylactic shock, she got out of bed and frantically scrabbled in her backpack for her auto-injector. Then, she remembered that she'd left it in her Amati case. She called the campus switchboard and was quickly connected to Jesse Montgomery's office. His phone rang and rang, its buzzing competing with the increasing ringing in Serena's ears. Realizing she had very little time left before she collapsed, Serena called 911. She tried desperately to gasp out who she was and what was happening.

At five-thirty, Patricia Stanley turned away from her laptop and picked up her cell phone. She dialed Serena's number, hoping she wouldn't actually wake her. Patricia heard Serena's recording, inviting the caller to leave a message. Well, maybe Serena was really sleeping deeply. Patricia tried the number again. Still Serena didn't answer. Now Patricia wasn't sure what to do. Maybe Serena really needed to sleep. Maybe she'd rather celebrate another night. On the other hand, Patricia had promised to wake her, and Serena might be annoyed if she didn't. Patricia decided she'd stop over at Serena's room and decide what to do then.

Patricia got off the elevator at Serena's floor and went down the hall to Serena's room. She knocked on the door, but got no answer. She knocked again, this time calling out, "Serena, it's Patricia. Wake up!" When she got no reply, she checked the bathroom.

Maybe Serena was there. A quick glance around the bathroom showed that nobody was there. Now Patricia was a little concerned. Where was Serena? Maybe Marcie would know.

Patricia got to Marcie's room to find the RA's door open and Marcie talking to the Residence Director. "Hey, Marcie," she said. "Do you know where Serena is?" Marcie turned towards Patricia. The minute she did, Patricia could see that something was very wrong.
"What's going on?" she asked with rising panic.
"It's Serena. She's been rushed to the hospital."
"What? Why? What happened?"
"She collapsed in her room. She must have called 911, because the paramedics came and rushed her away."
"When was this?"
"About an hour ago. She's at the hospital now. I couldn't go with her because I have to stay here and report on what happened. Tessa's with her, though."
"OK, thanks. I'm going right over."
"Call me when you know anything, OK?"
"I will."

A terrified Patricia fled down the stairs of Cooper Hall and rushed to the student parking lot next to the Student Union Building. Barely noticing anything, she jerked open the door of her Honda and, in a moment, was speeding towards Tilton General Hospital. As soon as she had parked, she jumped out of her car and hurried to the Emergency entrance. When she got to the Information desk, she said, "Is Serena Brinkman here?" Before the receptionist could answer, a voice called out, "Patricia! Over here!" Patricia turned and saw a white-faced Tessa Oliver waving to her from one of the chairs in the waiting area. She dashed over to Tessa and gasped, "What happened?"

Choking back tears, Tessa said, "I came back from class and there were paramedics in our room. They had her on a stretcher. They couldn't tell me for sure what was wrong, but they think it's anaphylactic shock. They said she'd called 911. It's been forty minutes and nobody's told me anything else."

For a few minutes the girls sat silently, their faces strained and exhausted from stress. Then, they saw a man in hospital scrubs walking towards them. Tessa nudged Patricia. "That's the doctor who was working on Serena," she hissed. The two

girls straightened up and went to meet him.
Maybe he could tell them something.

Chapter Seven

At ten o'clock the next morning, Joel
Williams left the classroom where he had
just finished with his Law Enforcement
Procedures class. Williams had been a
member of Tilton University's Department
of Criminal Justice for three years, having
chosen teaching as a second career. Prior to
that, he'd been a detective with the Tilton
Police Department for eighteen years. Now
in his early fifties, Williams was content
with his decision to move into higher
education. He enjoyed working with
students, and although academia certainly
had its disadvantages, even frustrations, he
had no regrets about his choice of a second
career.

When he got to his office, Williams saw a
student waiting by his door. One look at her
tear-stained face was enough to tell him that
something was terribly wrong. Patricia
Stanley, one of his advisees, was almost
always calm and usually under control. Now
she spoke in a choked voice. "Dr. Williams,
I really need to talk to you. Do you have
some time?"
"Of course, Patricia, come on in. Have a
seat. I was wondering why you weren't in
class today."

Williams unlocked his office door and Patricia followed him inside, sliding her backpack off and settling into a chair. She pulled a tissue out of her backpack and wiped her eyes. After a moment, she said, "Sorry, I know I'm falling to pieces here."

"It's all right. Take your time."

"Thanks. I think I'll be OK. But I wanted to let you know why I missed class, and that I'll be missing a few other classes. I hope I don't have to, but I might even have to ask for an Incomplete in your Law Enforcement Procedures class."

"What's going on?"

"Something awful's happened. Serena Brinkman – my partner – died yesterday. I'm just really broken up."

"I'm so sorry!" Williams said. "That's terrible! How long were you two together?"

"Almost two years. We were talking about staying together, you know, permanently."

"I know you two meant a lot to each other. And of course if you need an extension, we can work that out. Is there anything else I can do to help?"

"I don't know. I'm just so upset right now. She died so suddenly."

"What happened?"

"They said it was anaphylactic shock. Serena was severely allergic to peanuts or anything with peanut flour in it. They say she must have come into contact with something that triggered her allergies. She called 911, but they couldn't save her." With that, Patricia broke into tears. Williams silently handed her a box of tissues that he kept on his desk. She nodded her thanks and quickly blew her nose and wiped her face. Then, after drawing a ragged breath, she went on.

"The thing is, Dr. Williams, I just don't understand how Serena could possibly have gotten exposed to peanuts. She was always really careful. She read labels, the whole thing. She knew how dangerous it was for her to be around peanut dust or peanut flour."

"She might have been exposed accidentally. From what I know about peanut allergies, there's a risk of cross-contamination."

"I know that. Serena did, too. She always tried to be careful."

"I'm terribly sorry this happened, Patricia. Will you be going to the funeral?"

"Yeah, I will. That's the other thing I wanted to tell you. They don't know when the funeral will be, but I'll be out of town for a few days for it."

"That won't be a problem. You're a good student, and I'm sure you'll be able to catch up."

"Dr. Williams, there's something else."

Williams heard the sense of urgency in Patricia's voice. He looked at her more closely. "What's that?

"I don't think it was an accident."

"You mean, you think Serena deliberately exposed herself?"

"I don't know. I just know that she didn't take chances. She would not have knowingly eaten anything that had peanuts in it."

"So what are you saying?"

"I don't know what I'm saying. There's just something, well, wrong about this. Something just doesn't fit."

"Look, I can only guess how upset you must be. It's not a good idea to jump to conclusions, though. It's dangerous to do that. Do you have any reason to think that it wasn't an accident?"

"Not really. I don't know. It's just that she was careful. Especially yesterday. Serena was a violinist – a really talented one – and yesterday she won a major competition. One she'd been practicing for since the beginning of the semester. She wouldn't have risked her health like that. She just wouldn't. That competition was too important to her. "

"It could have been some kind of accident."

"Maybe, but I just don't think so."

"Well, when something like this happens, they do an autopsy. Serena's parents will get the results. Maybe they'll let you know what they are."

"They might. We're on good terms. I don't know, though…"

"Listen, Patricia, it's not a good idea to make wild guesses about what might have happened. Why not wait until the test results are in? They might give you the answers you want."

"I guess so. I just – I think there's something wrong about this, though. I really do. I know some of the people Serena hung around with. Maybe I could ask around?"

"I wouldn't do that. They won't be able to give you any medical information. Until you have that, you wouldn't even know what questions to ask. Why not wait for the test results."

"All right," Patricia said reluctantly. "But if there is something wrong, will you help me? You were a detective. You'll know what to do."

"I don't know that there's anything to detect. I think it's a matter of figuring out how Serena got exposed to peanuts, if that's what happened. But any time you want to talk, I'm here."

"Thanks." Patricia got up slowly and said, "You will help me, though, if - if this wasn't an accident, though, right?"

Silently telling himself he'd probably regret his answer, Williams said, "Let me know when you get any test results. We'll talk about it then. I'm not promising anything, but we'll see."

"All right. And thanks for listening. I really appreciate it."

Patricia wiped her face once more and blew her nose again. Then, having tossed the tissues into Williams' trash can, she picked up her backpack, thanked Williams again and left his office.

Williams devoted the next hour to answering his Email and rereading the manuscript of an article he planned to submit to the *Journal of Modern Criminal Detection*. He hated to admit it, even to himself, but Patricia Stanley had gotten him thinking. He was truly sorry that she'd lost someone special, and, from what she'd said, Serena's death had been sudden. Even when he was a detective, Williams had especially hated it when young people died needlessly. Now that he was around young people on a daily basis, he hated it even more. After a time, his thoughts were interrupted by his rumbling stomach. He hadn't eaten anything since six-thirty that morning. So he shut down his computer, pushed his chair back from the desk and stretched himself to his full six feet of height. He picked up his corduroy blazer from its hook on the back of his door and shrugged it on. Then, after locking the door behind him, he headed towards the Kozy Korner Kafe, where he often got his lunch.

Williams' path to the Kozy Korner took him past Lessner Hall. As he neared the building, he decided that his stomach could wait for ten minutes while he indulged his curiosity. Silently berating himself for being unable to resist, he went into the building. On one of the walls in the lobby, Williams noticed a large bulletin board labeled *Announcements and Accomplishments*. Patricia had mentioned that Serena had won an important competition; maybe there would be a notice about it. He headed to the bulletin board and, in a moment or two, saw a photograph of a young woman with a violin taking a bow. Under the photograph was the caption: *Sophomore Serena Brinkman named Concertmistress for the Young Artists' Orchestra*. Either nobody here knew that Serena was dead or, what was more likely, nobody had thought to take that notice down. Almost before he realized it, Williams wondered who this Serena Brinkman had beaten. From what he knew, music competitions were serious businesses. It would have been a real blow to someone else when Serena had won. Williams stopped in mid-thought. "That's what you get for being a cop for too long," he told himself. He shook his head in irritation and refocused his attention on his protesting stomach. It was definitely time for lunch.

Troy Brinkman drove through a late-morning fog towards his parents' home in Swarthmore. Earlier that morning, he had arranged to take some time off from his classes, and was planning to go with his family to Serena's funeral, and then spend a few days at home. As he drove, Troy mentally replayed the conversation he'd had late last night with Patricia Stanley. She had wanted to tell Troy about Serena's death right away, rather than have him hear about it from someone else, so she'd gotten his number from Serena's cell phone.

Patricia had told Troy that the doctors thought Serena had accidentally been exposed to something that had triggered a serious allergic reaction. They didn't know what she'd eaten or drunk that could have put her at risk, but Patricia had said that the only thing Serena was allergic to was peanuts and peanut flour. Troy had agreed with her. He didn't know of anything else, either, that would have caused Serena to have such a violent allergic reaction. As he thought about it now, Troy guessed that there would probably be an autopsy, but it wouldn't necessarily show the source of the allergen. Well, that wouldn't happen for a couple of days, so there was nothing to do but wait for the report.

From the medical details, Troy's thoughts turned to the larger question of what it would be like without Serena. He'd been Serena's friend as well as her cousin all his life, and he'd miss her very much. That hurt, and Troy's jaw tightened as he thought about how hard the next few weeks were going to be. He almost didn't want to make this trip, but he knew he had to. Once this was over, he could get on with his life. Almost against his will, Troy started thinking about Serena's trust fund. Her death meant that Troy wouldn't have to worry about money any more – at least for now. If he could just get through these next few weeks, things would definitely start to look up. He almost smiled as he headed towards the interstate that would take him to Swarthmore.

While Troy was on his way to his family, Michelle Park was sitting in the office of Timothy Morrow, Chair of the Department of Music. Morrow had called her in this morning saying he had something important to discuss with her.

"Thanks for coming in, Michelle," he began.

"Of course."

"I called you because you may or may not be aware of the tragedy that took place last night."

"Tragedy?"

"Yes. Serena Brinkman died very unexpectedly yesterday."

"That's terrible! How did it happen?"

"I don't have all of the details yet, of course, but I'm told that it was a serious allergic reaction."

"How awful!"

"Yes, it was. We'll have a memorial for her as soon as we hear from her parents about what they'd like to do. For now, though, there's something pressing I need to discuss with you – the Young Artists' Orchestra. Serena Brinkman's death means that the orchestra will need a concertmaster or concertmistress. I was just on the phone this morning with the Director of the orchestra. The jury awarded you second place in the competition, so you will be named concertmistress."

Michelle caught her breath. She wasn't quite sure how to react to what Dr. Morrow was saying. It wouldn't be appropriate to exult in the Director's decision, but at the same time, she didn't want to pretend to any deep sorrow. She'd liked Serena, and respected her talent, but they hadn't been friends. After a moment she said, "Thank you very much for telling me. Of course it's a real honor to be named concertmistress. I'm so sorry about Serena's death, though. It must be very hard on her family."

"I'm sure it must be. As I say, we'll be having a memorial for her here, and I'm sure her parents would appreciate your condolences.

"That's a good idea. I'll certainly get in touch with them. Let me know if there's anything else I can do."

"Thank you. For right now, just prepare to represent Tilton well during the orchestra's tour."

"I will. And thank you. I'll do my best."

"I know that you will."

After thanking the Chair again, Michelle left his office. She hurried back to her dorm room, where she immediately sat down on her bed, drew a long breath and pulled her cell phone out of her backpack. She was looking forward to calling her parents with this news.

Marcie Bratton watched the young women who lived on her floor file out of the lounge. She'd spent the last hour talking to them about Serena's death and answering their questions as best she could. When she'd announced the death last night, the residents had reacted with shock and horror at the news. They hadn't begun to process what had happened until this morning, so Marcie and the Residence Director had decided to hold a floor meeting today, so that everyone could air her concerns. Throughout the meeting, Marcie had tried her best to focus on what the girls were saying. It was the only way she could control her own feelings as the reality of what Serena's death would mean began to sink in.

As the last resident left the lounge, Marcie began to relax the firm grip she'd had on her own emotions. With Serena dead, there would be no need to worry. Except for Lenore Hughes, Serena had been the only one who'd known Marcie's secret. Now, Marcie would be safe – unless Serena had told Tessa or Patricia Stanley. Marcie would have to think about that, but for now, things would probably be all right. Tessa had gone home early this morning. She wouldn't likely be back for a week or so and when she came back, Marcie would find out what, if anything, she knew. As for Patricia, Marcie would have to hope that Serena hadn't said anything to her. If she had, Marcie would have to deal with that. She was going to have to find out – and soon – whether Patricia knew her secret. There was nothing she could do about that now, though. Patricia would be going home later today, so Marcie wouldn't have the chance to talk to her, either, until next week. For now, the best thing to do would be to stay calm and not overreact. The less attention she drew to herself, the better.

While Marcie cleaned up the lounge and prepared to go to her afternoon class, Jesse Montgomery was opening the safe in Department of Music's main office. He carefully drew out Serena Brinkman's Amati, and prepared to take it back to his office. He and the other faculty members had been called to an emergency department meeting this morning where Thomas Morrow had announced Serena's death. Though he wasn't proud of it, one of Montgomery's first thoughts had been about that Amati. He couldn't be sure, of course, but he guessed that Serena's family probably knew she had the Amati on campus, and at some point, would wonder what had happened to it. For now, though, they would be absorbed in their grief and loss, and might not miss it. He would have to think about what to do if the questions came, but at the moment, he was the only one on campus who knew where that Amati was. As he tucked the violin under his arm and closed the safe, Montgomery couldn't help the rush of sheer pleasure it gave him to have it in his possession. He took it up to his office and closed his door. Then, he opened the case, drew it out and laid it on his desk. He was sad about Serena's death; she'd been a nice girl and a talented artist. But to have this Amati gave him an exhilaration that he had rarely felt.

Tony Ferguson sat in his room, staring blankly at his computer screen. On it were the notes he'd written the day that he had interviewed Serena Brinkman for the *Vintage*. It had only been a week ago, but now it seemed much longer. Two hours ago, his editor had called him, telling him he would have to pull that interview from the material he was compiling for his article. Tony could still hear his editor's voice explaining why. Serena Brinkman was dead. Strangely enough, Serena's death still didn't seem real to Tony. There were his notes, and right next to them the picture he'd taken of her sitting on the bench the afternoon he'd interviewed her. He'd even started writing up the profile he'd been going to do. Now Serena was dead. Maybe it was better this way, though. In her pictures and in the notes, Serena was exactly what Tony wanted her to be. She was young, beautiful, and his. There was no need to worry about what she might do or think on her own. Yes, it was definitely better that Serena wasn't going to be difficult any more. With a grim smile, Tony saved his interview and carefully put the photographs away in a manila folder he'd labeled with Serena's name. He would keep her profile where he could see her whenever he wanted.

After he'd finished with his notes, Tony shut down his computer and packed his backpack. He had a class, and then he was planning to go over to the school's newspaper office. He was hoping they would use some pictures he'd taken of Harvest Day in their write-up about the festival. The more exposure his work got, the better chance he'd have for an internship at the Tilton *Sentinel* next fall. Every year, the *Sentinel* staff chose two promising Tilton University photography students for a semester-long internship that included riding along with *Sentinel* reporters and attending weekly workshops. Interns who did good work got strong recommendations for full-time positions at area newspapers. Tony even knew of a few interns who'd gotten jobs at the big papers in Philadelphia, Baltimore and Pittsburgh. Now that he was a junior, Tony wanted to take advantage of as many internships, special events, and freelancing as he could. Once he made his name as a photographer, women would stop turning him down. Women like Serena. She'd never have treated him the way she did if she'd known how talented he was. Well, that didn't matter now. Serena would never treat him disrespectfully again. Neither would those other women who'd been protecting her. Serena was dead and Tony Ferguson was going to be a world-famous photographer who could have any woman he wanted. The thought cheered him as he packed his backpack and headed off to class.

By five o'clock that afternoon, Patricia Stanley had finished making arrangements to be out of town for a few days. She was glad that her professors had been so understanding about her absence. Patricia was a conscientious student who rarely missed class and took her work seriously. Now, she sat in her dorm room, looking at her opened suitcase. Soon, she'd zip it up and be on her way to Devon, where she would spend a few days with Serena's family.

 She'd thought about flying back to Malibu, but no one would be there. Her father and stepmother had booked a cruise to celebrate their wedding anniversary, and they'd left two days before. They didn't even know yet that Serena was dead. Besides, October was the worst month of the year to be in Malibu; the ever-present danger of wildfires was at its greatest during Santa Ana season, when the hot winds blew west from the desert and the sky would sometimes be choked with smoke. More than once, Patricia and her family had come close to being evacuated, and she'd sworn that, as soon as she was able, she would move away from wildfire country. So now, she felt no particular wish to go home. It would be better for her to be in Devon, where she could be with other people who'd loved Serena. As she zipped up her suitcase and glanced around her room to make sure she hadn't forgotten anything, Patricia thought about how lucky she was that she got along well with Serena's parents. They would need each other right now.

At five-thirty that evening, Joel Williams pulled his Dodge sedan into the garage. It was going to be a cool, crisp night, and he was looking forward to using the fireplace for the first time this season. He noticed that his wife, Laura, hadn't come home yet. Williams quickly got out of his car, crossed the garage and the driveway to the mailbox and scooped up the day's mail. He walked slowly back towards the garage, flipping through the mail as he went. When he got into the garage, Williams pushed the garage door button and let himself into the house as the garage door hummed shut behind him. He'd no sooner put his key in the lock when he heard his friendly mutt, Oscar, barking a happy greeting.

"Hey, boy, how are you?" Williams asked as he fended off Oscar's excited jumps. He gave the dog a few pets, and then leashed him in preparation for a walk. The two then set off around the block for their early-evening ritual. By the time they returned, Laura had gotten home and was opening the mail that Joel had left on the coffee table in the living room.

"How was your day?" she asked as her husband unleashed Oscar and hung up his jacket.

"Busy, but not bad. I didn't get as much done as I wanted to, but then-"

"- you never do."

Joel smiled; Laura really did understand him. He kissed her and asked, "How was your day?"

"Pretty frustrating, actually. I was all ready to go on three of our cases, and all three got continued." Laura Williams was an Assistant District Attorney, and very meticulous about her work. She prepared thoroughly for each case, and didn't like to feel that her efforts were wasted.

"Tell me what happened."

With that cue, Laura detailed her day while Joel settled onto the comfortable, overstuffed sofa beside her. When she'd finished, she noticed that Joel's attention had strayed.

"You're a million miles away, Joel. What are you thinking about?"

"Sorry! I was listening. It's just that when you were talking about that poisoning case, it made me think of something that happened today."

"What happened?"

"Well, your defendant allegedly poisoned her husband for his life insurance money.

The defense is saying it was accidental overdose, since the victim was taking medication. That made me think of something one of my advisees was telling me about today. It seems her partner just died – very suddenly – from an acute allergic reaction."

"And you think maybe that death wasn't accidental?"

"I don't know. Apparently this girl – the victim – was severely allergic to peanuts and peanut flour, and Patricia Stanley – that's my advisee – said that she was always very careful to avoid that kind of thing. But last night, she died of anaphylactic shock. Patricia doesn't see how she could have been exposed."

"Well, that might happen to anyone. Lots of products have peanut flour in them, don't they? Maybe she just didn't know she was being exposed."

"Well, that's what I said, but Patricia thinks there was something wrong about the death."

"Sounds pretty far-fetched to me. Maybe this girl is just overwrought. Blame's a really common way to deal with grief."

"I know."

"But you think maybe Patricia's right?"

"I don't know. I really don't. But I do know that Patricia Stanley's a pretty sensible kid.

She's not a drama queen, and she's good at focusing on the facts. If she says something's wrong, it's because she really thinks so, not because she's going there instead of dealing with her grief."

"Well, I'm really sorry to hear that someone so young died. That's hard on the family, and must be hard on your advisee. It's no wonder she's wants to know how it happened. I'll bet she and the family have lots of questions. We have a good ME, though, so I'm sure they'll be able to get some closure."

"Yeah, you're probably right. I just hate it when kids die."

"Me, too. So what did you say to Patricia – that's the name, right?"

"Yeah, Patricia Stanley. I told her pretty much the same thing you just said. The medical report will probably answer her questions. Until then, she's taking a few days off, going to the funeral and spending time with the family."

"Sounds sensible."

"Yeah, like I said, she's a pretty solid kid. She's got her head screwed on right."

"That's good. So how was the rest of your day?"

Joel filled Laura in on his classes and the day's meetings as the two of them went into the kitchen to get started with dinner. Laura put the radio on as they began to chop the vegetables and meat for stir-fry. They both liked to keep up with community events, and neither wanted to miss the six o'clock news. As they began to cook, the announcer said, "Coming up, all of today's news, but first, these upcoming community events. This Saturday at seven o'clock, Tilton University will sponsor a special preview of this year's Young Artists' Orchestra, featuring piano soloist Artemio Rodriguez, and concertmistress Michelle Park. The Young Artists' Orchestra is made up of the finest musical artists at local colleges and universities who compete for positions, so this weekend's performance should be a real treat. Also, don't miss the Tilton High School Drama Club's performance of *Twelve Angry Men*......."

Williams didn't pay close attention to the rest of the broadcast. In his mind, he saw the photo at Lessner Hall announcing that Serena Brinkman, the dead girl, had originally been named concertmistress. Whoever this Michelle Park was, she'd just gotten a real coup, from what Williams understood about orchestras. All of a sudden, Laura's voice pulled him back to the present.

"Joel, you've got that faraway look again. What's up?"

"Nothing. Sorry. Just thinking about that poor kid again. She was supposed to be concertmistress in that orchestra they were just talking about, that's all."

"Damned shame."

"Yeah, it is. It's hard not to think about it."

"I know. That's part of what makes you good at what you do. You care. Now come on, let's eat before this gets cold. There's nothing you can do about that kid's death."

"You're absolutely right." Joel gave his wife a quick hug, and then they both turned their attention to eating.

Chapter Eight

The knock on the Brinkmans' door came at nine o'clock in the morning. When their maid opened it, two Tilton police detectives, Alex Logan and Dan Foster, showed their badges and asked to speak to the Brinkmans. The visibly shaken maid ushered them into the living room and said she'd tell the Brinkmans they were there. Five minutes later, Spencer Brinkman came into the room. "What can I do for you, Officers? This is really not a very good time. We're trying to make arrangements for our daughter's funeral."

"We're very sorry for your loss, Mr. Brinkman," said Logan, "But we have a few questions and it would really help us do our job if you'd give us a few minutes."

"Questions? What do you mean?"

"We'd like you and Mrs. Brinkman to tell us a little bit more about your daughter."

"Well...I suppose...- what's this all about? The doctor who told us about – about Serena told us she died of a severe allergic reaction. Isn't that what happened?"

"Why don't you ask Mrs. Brinkman to join us, and we'll get through this as quickly as we can," said Foster.

There was no need for that; Natalie Brinkman had heard the doorbell and come downstairs to see what was going on. Now she came slowly into the room. Her face was drawn and her eyes were red; it was obvious she'd been crying.

"I'm Natalie Brinkman. What's going on?"

"Please sit down, Mrs. Brinkman. I'm Detective Logan and this is Detective Foster – Tilton PD. We'd like to ask you a few questions."

The Brinkmans sat down slowly on the couch. Spencer Brinkman's face was hard, his wife's anxious. When they'd settled themselves, Logan continued.

"The reason we're here is that we have reason to think that your daughter's death was not accidental."

"What?" Spencer Brinkman half rose from his seat and then, recalling himself, sat back down. "What are you talking about?'

"We got the preliminary report from the medical examiner's office. The girls who were with your daughter at the hospital told the doctors she was allergic to peanuts and peanut flour. Is that right?"

"That's right. She – she was." said Natalie Brinkman.

"Was she aware of this allergy?"

"Yes, of course," Natalie answered. "We've known about it since Serena was a little girl.

She was always really careful to avoid anything with peanuts, and she always had her auto-injector – just in case."

"Well, the ME's office found a very high concentration of the proteins found in peanut flour in her system. They think that's what caused Serena's death."

Natalie Brinkman stared at the two police officers for a moment. Then, she slowly said, "Are you suggesting that Serena committed suicide?"

"We're not really suggesting anything, Ma'am," said Foster. "We just want to know what was going on in Serena's life. In cases like your daughter's, where the coroner can't really establish manner of death, we have to ask questions."

"I can tell you this," put in Spencer Brinkman, "Serena didn't commit suicide. She came home for a visit two weeks before – before she died. She was fine then. She was happy, she was enjoying life, and she was looking forward to a music competition she was getting ready for."

At the mention of the competition, Natalie Brinkman lowered her head and wiped her eyes with a tissue she'd been holding. Her husband patted her shoulder and then continued. "She was looking forward to life, Detectives. She had no reason to kill herself."

"No money problems? Grade problems? Love problems?"

"No!"

Foster looked at his partner and then delicately said, "Sometimes, well, college students don't exactly tell their parents everything going on in their lives. Is it possible there might have been something going on that Serena wouldn't tell you?"

All of a sudden, another voice broke into the conversation, startling everyone.

"I can tell you whatever you want to know." Patricia Stanley had come into the living room. Now she sat in an easy chair and said, "You're cops, right? What do you want to know?"

"Yes, we're with the Tilton Police Department. Can you tell us who you are?" asked Logan.

"I'm Patricia Stanley. I'm - I was – Serena's partner. We were at Tilton together, and we were going to stay together after college. I knew her about as well as anyone."

"What can you tell us about her? Was anything going on in her life that we ought to know about?"

"No! That's what's so strange. She was getting decent grades, she wasn't upset about anything. There was no reason at all for her to kill herself. None!"

Again, the two police officers exchanged glances. "Um… you two weren't having any problems, were you?" asked Foster.

"No – really! We were happy together. We – we were going to stay together."

"You're sure there was nothing going on to upset Serena?"

"Yes! And I'd have known, too."

Logan had been making notes as Patricia talked with his partner. Now, he said, "Anybody else you know who could tell us something about Serena?"

'Well," said Natalie, "There was her roommate, Tessa."

"That's right," Patricia agreed, "Tessa and Serena were friends. I don't think she can tell you anything that I can't, but you could talk to her."

"Good. Thanks. We'll do that, then," said Logan.

With that, the two detectives rose and thanked Patricia and the Brinkmans for their time. As they were preparing to leave, Patricia asked, "Do you think Serena was murdered?"

Spencer said sharply, "Patricia!" and Natalie gasped. Patricia turned to them.

[171]

"Look, I'm sorry. I'm going through hell, too, but Serena did not kill herself. There was no reason for her to commit suicide. And she was always really careful about her diet. So an accident just doesn't make sense. So if she didn't kill herself and this wasn't an accident, then someone killed her."

Foster said, "Look, Ms. – Stanley? I can only imagine how upset you must be. But we can't jump to conclusions. Right now we're just trying to find out what happened to your friend. We have a long way to go to figure out why Serena died. Your best bet is to let us do our jobs. We'll talk to Serena's roommate, we'll look at the ME's complete report, and we'll get answers. But right now, it's way too early to assume this was a murder."

"He's right, Patricia," said Spencer.

"I know you have to do your jobs," Patricia answered, "And I don't want to get in your way or tell you what to do. But Serena did not die naturally, and I want to know why."

"You will. You, too, Mr. and Mrs. Brinkman," said Logan. Then the two detectives took their leave after promising to call when they found out any new information.

After Logan and Foster had gone, Spencer Brinkman asked, "Patricia, what makes you think Serena was murdered? Do you know something we don't?"

"No, or I'd have said something. It's just that I can't think of anything else that makes sense."

"It can't be murder," Natalie Brinkman said. "Why would anybody want to kill Serena? She had no enemies. Everyone loved her!"

"For right now, let's just drop it," Spencer said. "We're all upset. Let's just wait for the police and the coroner to find out what happened."

Patricia wasn't at all interested in letting anything drop, but she didn't want to upset the Brinkmans; they'd always been good to her. Besides, they and the cops had a point. Still, although she'd meant what she said about not getting in the way of the police, Patricia was more and more convinced that something was very, very wrong about Serena's death.

The next morning, Tessa Oliver sat on the end of her bed in her dorm room. Facing her was a police officer from the Tilton Police Department. Tessa had been assigned to a new dorm room when she returned to campus, and had just finished unpacking when the detectives had knocked on her door. Now, she ran her hand abstractedly through her thick, tousled black hair. "I don't know how this could have happened," she said.

"Was Serena in the habit of watching what she ate?" This came from Detective Alex Logan, who'd come to find out what he could from Serena Brinkman's roommate.

"Oh, absolutely! She watched everything she ate, and she was a fanatic about reading labels. There is no way that she would accidentally have eaten anything with peanuts in it. She was too careful."

"It sounds as though you don't think this was an accident."

"I don't know what happened. I really don't. I can tell you this, though. Serena didn't even take fries from other people's fast food bags. She was really careful."

"Well, then let me ask you this. Can you think of any reason she might have deliberately eaten peanuts?"

"On purpose? And risk killing herself - oh! You mean suicide? No!"

"She wasn't having any problems? No worries?"

"None. I mean, she was having a tough time with chemistry, but she was passing it with no problem."

"No love problems? Money problems?"

"No not that, either. She and Patricia – did you talk to her? – were doing great, and Serena's rich. She never worried about money."

"No family trouble?"

"No, not that I know of. She went home a few times after the semester started, and she said she had a good time. Look, I just can't think of any reasons she'd want to kill herself."

"One more question, and I'm going to need you to be completely honest. You were Serena Brinkman's roommate. Did you ever see her using drugs? Any drinking?"

"Look, I'm not going to lie and say that Serena never drank anything. But she wasn't a heavy drinker – nothing like that. Once in a while a glass of wine or something, but that's it. She didn't use drugs, either. Not even weed."

"All right, we appreciate what you have told us. Here's my card. Just let me know if anything occurs to you, OK?"

"Yeah, sure," Tessa took the business card that Logan had offered her, and tucked it into her wallet. Then, Logan thanked her for her time and left. Tessa stared after him, more confused than ever about Serena's death.

At about the time that Tessa was talking to Logan, Patricia Stanley was pulling into the parking lot of the Tilton police station. She'd had a long drive through a steady autumn rain, but she'd barely noticed the weather. Since the detectives had left the Brinkman house the day before, Patricia hadn't been able to shake the thought that Serena's death had been deliberate. She'd been distracted the rest of the day trying to imagine who would want to kill Serena. Fortunately, she'd been planning to return to Tilton this morning, so she could occupy herself with packing and taking leave of the Brinkmans. It wasn't until she was halfway to Tilton that an idea had occurred to her. Now she wanted to let the police know as soon as she could.

Patricia got out of her car and flipped the hood of her windbreaker up over her head. Then, she strode purposefully inside the building and over to the receptionist's desk.
"May I help you?"
"Yes, thank you. Is Detective….Logan here? Or Detective Foster?"
"Let me see. Can I give them your name?"
"Yes, it's Patricia Stanley."
"OK, just a minute."
A moment or two later, Dan Foster opened the door that separated the waiting area of

the police station from the offices. Immediately he recognized the young woman he and his partner had met yesterday.

"Ms.....Stanley, right?"

"Yes, I'm Patricia Stanley. We met yesterday."

"That's right. How can I help you?"

"Well, you and Detective Logan told us to get in touch with you if there was anything we could tell you about Serena Brinkman's death. I had an idea this morning, and I wanted to tell you about it as soon as I could."

"OK, come on back to my desk."

Once the two of them had reached Foster's desk area, they took seats and Foster looked expectantly at his visitor. "So, you were telling me you had an idea about Serena Brinkman's death."

"Yes, it's just this. Like I said yesterday, I know she wasn't unhappy. She didn't have any reason to kill herself. Really. And she was too careful to have had an accident. That leaves murder, doesn't it?"

"That's really rushing things. We don't know that your friend was murdered. We're just asking questions right now."

"But I know she didn't kill herself and I'm sure there was no accident."

Foster was beginning to be a little irritated with this determined girl. You didn't just assume every case you saw was a murder. He found himself wishing that young people didn't watch as many cop shows as they did. Still, he was a fair man, and if the girl knew something, he wanted to know, too. "We're still looking into that, but go on. Do you know of anyone who would have wanted to kill your friend?"

"I wouldn't have thought so. But on the way here this morning, I was thinking of Tony Ferguson."

"Who's that?"

"This guy – he's a Tilton student and a photographer for the *Vintage*. That's our yearbook. He was crazy about Serena, but she turned him down. She didn't want to have anything to do with him."

"And you think he killed her?"

"I don't know. I really don't. I mean, he's kind of creepy, and he kept bugging Serena, but he never threatened her. And I'm not saying for sure that he did kill her. I'm just saying he's the only one I could think at the moment who would have a reason."

Foster noted Tony's name on the memo pad he kept by his telephone. Then he said, "OK, I've got that down. Anything else you can think of?"

"Not at the moment. But I really don't think Serena poisoned herself, and I just can't see her being careless enough for this to be an accident."

"Like I said, Ms. Stanley, we're asking questions, and we're going to get answers. I'm glad you came in with this, though. It's going to be helpful."

Feeling somewhat patronized, Patricia said, "So are you going to treat this as a murder, or not?"

"What we're not going to do is jump to conclusions. I promise that we'll get answers, though."

Now it was Patricia's turn to be irritated. She'd tried to be helpful, and it was occurring to her that this cop wasn't taking her very seriously. "You don't believe me, do you?" she slowly said.

"I'm not saying that. I'm saying we need to do our jobs. Part of our job is to look at all the possibilities, at least for now."

Patricia realized that it would do her no good to start an argument with this detective. It was clear that they didn't consider Serena's death a murder, and she hadn't been able to change anyone's mind. She also realized that she wouldn't do her case any good by making a scene about it. Still, it upset her to think that she was being dismissed.

"Look," she finally said, "I'm not crazy. I also know you have to do your job – I'm a criminal justice major, so I know you can't just go around accusing people of murder. But I know that Serena didn't kill herself, and I just can't believe she'd have come into contact with peanut flour by accident. She was too cautious for that."

Foster hadn't known this young woman was a crim. major. That might make things even worse. Young people always thought they knew more than they did until they'd been in the force for a while. At the same time, he didn't want to be rude. So he said, "I'm glad you realize we have to do our jobs, Ms. Stanley. Honestly, as soon as we know something, we will be in touch."

Forced to be satisfied with that response, Patricia thanked Foster for his time. She slowly left the building and, ducking her head against the rain, headed back to her car. She drove back to her dorm building, got her luggage out of the trunk and took it upstairs to her room. When she got there, she spent the next twenty minutes unpacking. Then she sat down on her bed and thought for a few moments. Finally, she nodded to herself, put her windbreaker back on and tucked her wallet, room key and student ID into the pocket of her jeans. She was going to need some help.

Carlton Hall, which housed Tilton University's Department of Criminal Justice, was a ten-minute walk from Patricia's dorm. She was so intent on her purpose, though, that she almost didn't notice the irritating rain. She automatically flipped up the hood of her windbreaker and hunched over as the rain began to fall more heavily. By the time she got to Carlton Hall, Patricia was nearly soaked, but she didn't care. Once inside the building, she peeled off her jacket, tossed her hair out of her face and shook the water off herself as best she could. Then she climbed the stairs to her destination on the third floor.

"C'mon in," called Joel Williams, "It's not locked." He glanced up from his desk to see who'd been knocking so insistently.
Patricia strode in, sat down briskly and said, "You said you would help me, right?"
"Oh, hi, Patricia. Do you mean with your work? I know you've been away for a few days," Williams hedged.
"No. I mean with Serena's death."
"Patricia, we talked about this, don't you remember? Whenever there's an unexplained death, the police and the coroner's office work together to find out

what happened. We've got some good professionals here in Tilton. We need to let them do their jobs. They'll find out what happened."

"I know they're investigating, but they think Serena killed herself. They're looking for the wrong kinds of things. I even went there this morning and told them I thought she might have been murdered, but the detective didn't believe me. Didn't you tell us in class about manner of death? There's accident, there's natural, there's suicide and there's homicide, right?"

"That's right."

"Well, they think this is suicide or accident, so they're not looking for suspects! I need your help convincing the police that Serena was murdered."

"How do you know it wasn't suicide or accident, Patricia? These things do happen."

"I know that! But like I told the detective, Serena wasn't depressed, or broke, or failing, or on drugs or booze or anything. She didn't have a crazy secret life. She had just won a major competition. She had no motive for suicide."

"OK, let's say you're right. What about accident?" Williams was getting interested now, despite his better judgment.

"No way! Patricia was as careful as… I don't know what. She read labels, she watched what she ate, the whole thing. I'm not saying it's absolutely impossible, but honest, Dr. Williams, she wasn't careless. She even carried her auto-injector everywhere."

Williams thought for a moment. If this Serena Brinkman was as careful as Patricia said she was, then anaphylactic shock by accident didn't make a lot of sense. And it did seem strange that someone with looks, money, talent, and a partner would have a reason to commit suicide. "Her grades ok in school?" he asked. "She get along with her family?"

"Yes, all of that was fine. She had no reason to be depressed or anything. Really."

"OK, look," Williams said, "The best thing you can do right now is to let the police do their jobs. If Serena was murdered, they'll find out who did it. But to have a murder, you have to have somebody who wanted the victim dead. Is there anyone who wanted Serena dead?"

"So you're going to help me?" Patricia looked eagerly into Williams' impassive face.

"I'm making no promises. But it wouldn't hurt if I knew as much as possible about the people in Serena's life."

Forgetting herself for a moment, Patricia jumped up from her seat and hugged Williams. "Thank you!" she smiled.

"All right now, sit back down. I can't help you if you don't tell me everything you know."

"Yeah, of course – sorry. Well, Serena had a lot of friends – people she know."

"Was there anyone who scared her? Threatened her? Got angry with her? Patricia answered, "Well, there was Tony Ferguson. I told the detective about him."

"What do you mean? Who's Tony Ferguson?"

"Well, he's this guy who works for the *Vintage* – you know, the yearbook. He was doing an article on Serena, and he was getting obsessed with her. I mean, he was practically stalking her."

"He ask her out or anything?"

"Yeah. Of course, she said, 'no,' but he wasn't happy about it."

"Did he threaten her or anything?"

"Well, one day he showed up in the basement of her dorm while she was doing laundry. Really scared the hell out of her. He didn't threaten her or hurt her, but he kept saying she'd change her mind and go out with him. He was really weird about her."

"OK, so Tony Ferguson. Who else? Anyone you can think of?"

Patricia sat silently for a moment. "No. I can't think of anyone. I mean, there was her rival for the competition. Her name's Michelle Park. But they were music rivals, not enemies. I mean, they even had a sundae one day together at Sweet Dreams, where I work. They didn't seem to be fighting or anything then."

"Fair enough. Anyone else?"

"No, I don't think so."

"OK, did you tell the detective any of this?"

"No, and I feel really stupid now, because he even asked me if I knew anything else. I guess I just got so flustered I wasn't thinking."

"Well, you're thinking now. So let me ask you, was there anything Serena had that someone might have wanted?"

"You mean somebody could have killed her for her money or something? I don't know much about her trust fund, really. She used it when she needed to pay tuition or something, but I don't know who gets it now. Maybe her parents know that."

"Maybe. If they do, the police will find out. Anything else you can tell me?'

"I don't think… wait! Yes, there was. She had this really rare violin."

"Violin?" asked Dan Foster. He was sitting in his cramped office cubicle, talking on the telephone with Serena Brinkman's mother.

"Yes," Natalie Brinkman answered. "It was a genuine Amati – a very valuable violin. She had it with her on campus, and when we – we emptied her room, it wasn't there. You asked us to call you if we thought of anything, and I just realized we never got the Amati."

"Do you have any idea what might have happened to it?"

"None at all. She told us she kept it locked in the dorm's safe unless she was using it. It might still be there, but they told us at the dorm that they'd given us all of her things."

"Do you have a picture of it?"

"Yes. We had it taken for insurance coverage. I could Email you the picture if you'd like."

"That'd be real helpful. Is there anyone who might have known about it?"

"Nobody in particular. Probably only someone in the Music Department would have known about it, though. I mean, she wouldn't have gone around telling people about it, right?"

'Probably not. I appreciate your telling about this, Mrs. Brinkman. As soon as I get the picture, we'll follow up, and we'll do the best we can to track it down. When we do, we'll see that you get it."

Natalie Brinkman wrote down the Email address Foster gave her, thanked him and then hung up. She turned to her husband and said, "I told them about the Amati. They said they'll do what they can to get it back to us."

"Good," said Spencer Brinkman. Then, he slowly said, "Natalie, do you think Patricia was right? That this was murder?'

"You mean because of the Amati? But it was a college campus, and not a Julliard or a Peabody. Would anyone know what it was?"

"They might if Serena told them."

"Oh, Spencer, that wasn't like her at all! She didn't flaunt her money. We didn't raise her that way."

"That's true….you're right, of course."

"Of course. Now, let me Email that picture of it before I forget." But secretly, they both began to wonder if there was something in what Patricia Stanley had said. Maybe Serena had been murdered.

At the Tilton police station, Dan Foster slowly hung up the phone and straightened up. He ran his fingers through his neatly trimmed afro, took off the wire-rimmed

[187]

reading glasses that he used for computer work, and went in search of his partner. He found Alex Logan at the coffee machine down the hall from their desks.

"Hey, get one for me, too, OK?"

"You paying this time?"

"You still owe me from yesterday!"

"All right, all right. Here. You take this one and I'll get another one."

When Logan had finished getting coffee for both of them, they went off in search of their boss, Captain Bert Schneider. As usual, Schneider was in his office, trying vainly to catch up on paperwork.

"You guys need me?" he asked when they appeared at his open door.

"Yeah, you asked us to stop by and update you on that Brinkman case."

"Oh, yeah, come on in."

Logan and Foster went into their boss' office and took seats. Schneider said, "So fill me in." With that, the two detectives told Schneider about their conversations with Serena Brinkman's parents, girlfriend and roommate. "From all we can tell," Foster said, "this girl had no reason to kill herself. She wasn't unhappy, there was nothing terrible going on in her life. By all accounts, she was happy with her life."

"That's right," added Logan. "We found no history of depression, no suicides in the family, nothing that would make us think she killed herself."

"So you guys think it was an accident?"

"Might have been," said Foster. "But I'm not sure. Seemed like she was pretty careful. Besides, the ME's office says that the only food she had within the ten hours before she died was a salad. And it wasn't one of those salads with nuts in them. It was just your basic salad – with ranch dressing. We don't know where she got it from, but it doesn't seem like it's the kind of thing that would be contaminated with peanuts from something else. Still, you never know."

"OK, what else do you guys have?"

'Tell him about the Amati, Dan," Logan said. So Foster did.

When the detectives had finished, Schneider said, "OK, find that Amati. We need to get it back to the parents. Try to find out, too, where this Brinkman girl ate, whether she might have accidentally gotten peanut flour. I want this off our desks."

This was Logan's and Foster's cue to let Schneider get back to work, and they were quick to respond. Logan said, "Got it," and the two detectives left Schneider's office. They returned to their own desks, where Foster printed out the picture Natalie

Brinkman had sent him. Then he and Logan put together their plan. They decided to start with the Department of Music. Serena Brinkman was a gifted violinist, so she probably spent a lot of time there; maybe somebody would know about the Amati. Who knows? They might even find out how she'd gotten that salad.

At Lessner Hall, Sergei Berzin was sitting in his office with his protégée, Michelle Park. They'd been discussing some of the pieces that the Young Artists' Orchestra would be playing on its tour, and Berzin had been offering Michelle some advice about making the most of this opportunity. They both looked up when they heard the knock on Berzin's doorframe.

'Dr. Sergei Berzin?"

"Yes, that is my name. How can I help you?"

"I'm Detective Logan and this is Detective Foster. We have a few questions about one of your advisees, Serena Brinkman."

Michelle murmured something about needing to practice and was about to leave, but Foster's raised hand stopped her.

"Just a minute, please, Miss. What's your name?"

"Michelle Park. I'm a student."

"Did you know Serena Brinkman?"

"Yes, she was a violin performance major, too. It's terrible that she's dead."

"Does either of you know about an Amati violin that she had?" asked Logan. "

Michelle nodded, and Sergei Berzin said, "Yes, I have seen it. She used it once in a while."

"Either of you seen it lately?"

"No," said Michelle. "The last time I saw it was the day of the competition for the Young Artists' Orchestra."

"I, too, saw it then, but not since," said Berzin. "But perhaps you should speak to my colleague, Dr. Jesse Montgomery. His office is next to mine. He is an expert on instruments, and he might know what happened to that violin. Serena told me he was very much interested in using it for a paper he was writing."

"Thank you. We'll do that. By the way, is there a cafeteria in this building, or a deli nearby?"

"Well," said Michelle, "there are a few places to eat in the Student Union Building, but not here at Lessner. Since you're not students, you'll have to pay in cash or with a card, but it's not expensive."

"Thanks. That's really helpful." The two detectives thanked Berzin and his student, and went to Jesse Montgomery's office next door.

When they got to his office and introduced themselves, Montgomery welcomed them and invited them to take seats. Foster said, "Thanks for your time. We appreciate it."

"What's this about?" Montgomery asked.

"You know about Serena Brinkman's death, right?"

"Yes, of course. Terrible tragedy!"

"Well, it turns out she had a very valuable Amati violin here on campus. Looked like this." Logan proffered the printout of the photo. "Serena's parents tell us it wasn't among her things when they cleaned out her room. Do you happen to know anything about it?"

"I knew she had an Amati. I believe she played it the day of the competition – the Young Artists' Orchestra competition. That picture does look like the instrument, too. I don't know what happened to it, though."

"We understand you were interested in it for a paper you're writing?"

"I asked her about it, yes, but – so sad! – she died before she let me borrow it. Is – is there anything else?"

"No, thanks. Mind if we keep in touch if anything comes up?"

"No – no, of course not. I really must go now – meetings and classes, you understand."

"Sure, no problem. We understand how busy you are," Logan said.

Montgomery got up quickly, murmured a goodbye and walked with the detectives to the door of his office. He carefully closed and locked the door and headed towards the elevator. Logan and Foster followed more slowly.

"That guy is nervous," Logan said.

"Yeah, he is. Might be he just gets weird around cops. Lot of people do."

"Could be. Maybe not. I'd like to take a look around his stuff, though. If he's an expert on instruments, it could be that he took the Amati. He'd know how valuable it is."

"That's kind of a leap, but you might be right. Let's talk to Montgomery again – see if he'll tell us anything else."

"OK, let's go find him."

An hour and a half later, Jesse Montgomery dismissed his Music Theory I students and slid his lecture notes into his briefcase. He glanced around the room to be sure he hadn't left anything. Then, he left the

[193]

classroom and went down a flight of stairs at the end of the hall. He pushed open the stairwell door and, directly across from that door, stopped to unlock another door. This led to a small music laboratory that Montgomery had set up two years before for his instrument analyses. It wasn't as well-equipped as he'd have liked – the department budget didn't allow for extravagance, and the National Endowment for the Arts grant he'd gotten hadn't been generous. Still, he was pleased to have his own space for his work. Now he flicked on the light, closed the door behind him and crossed the room to the opposite wall where there was a built-in wall cabinet. Montgomery drew a key out of his pocket and unlocked the cabinet. He reached in and drew out a violin case. He carefully opened it and smiled at the reassuring sight of the honey-brown violin glowing from its blue velvet resting place. He closed the case carefully and then snapped the clasps. He lifted up the violin and picked up his briefcase. Again, he crossed the room and opened the door. He was startled to see two men on the other side of it.

"Detectives! I didn't hear you knock. How – how did you find me?"

"Sorry if we startled you, Dr. Montgomery. We just got here. The department secretary said you might be here. She said you usually come here to work after your classes."

"I see. Well, I thought we already talked, Detectives. Was there anything else you wanted to know?"

"We're still curious about Serena Brinkman's Amati violin. We'd like to return it to her family, so if there's anything else you could tell us about it, that'd be really helpful."

"As I said before, I did see it, but I don't know where it is now. So, if you'll excuse me, I've got to –"

"– Dr. Montgomery, we know you're busy, but we really need to find that violin. The department secretary said that you keep a lot of rare instruments here. That's why we thought it might be here. Mind if we take a look around?"

"You're welcome to look, but it's not here," Montgomery said, almost belligerently.

"That'd be great," Logan said. "How about we start with the case you're carrying?"

"This? This is my personal violin. It's not the one you're looking for."

"Well, good. If we can just take a quick look at it, we'll know the Amati isn't here."

"Look, I really don't have time for–"

"Please, Dr. Montgomery. It would really help us."

Montgomery quickly thought about his options. After a long moment, he sighed deeply and said, "Gentlemen, this is very awkward for me. You see, I'm doing a study of antique violins. I asked Serena – Ms. Brinkman – if she would lend me her Amati. She agreed, and we arranged for her to drop it off after her performance in the competition. I never got the chance to give it back to her."

"And that's the Amati?"

"Well, yes it is. I just – I wanted to keep it safe. Not leave it lying around here."

"We'd like to take a look, please."

Unwillingly, Montgomery handed the violin case to Logan, who placed it on a nearby worktable. Foster stepped over and opened the case. "Yup," he said. "That's the Amati." Then he returned to Montgomery, who had sat heavily down on a stool drawn up to another worktable.

"Dr. Montgomery, it doesn't look good that you lied to us about this. Mind explaining yourself?"

"I just – it was a once-in-a-lifetime chance to really have an Amati. Does either of you realize what that means? I know it was foolish. Maybe even illegal. I just couldn't resist it – I just couldn't!" Montgomery slowly dropped his head into his hands.

While he'd been talking, Logan had been looking through the case. All of a sudden, he said, "Hey, Foster." Foster glanced over at him, and Logan jerked his head in the direction of the violin case's opened accessory compartment. Foster quickly crossed over to Logan to see what Logan wanted to show him. There, buried under a set of replacement strings, was an auto-injector.

"Safety cap's off," murmured Logan. "Needle's out, too. I'm no expert, but I'm pretty sure that means this was used."

Foster nodded. In an equally low-pitched voice, he said, "Hospital report said she died there. No epinephrine in her blood, either. I think we need to have a longer conversation with this guy."

He walked back over to Montgomery and said, "Dr. Montgomery, we have a few more questions we'd like to ask you. We'd like you to come with us down to the police station, where we can talk."

"What? Am I under arrest? I didn't really steal the violin! I mean, she died. I couldn't return it. What was I supposed to do?"

"Right now, you're not under arrest. We just want to ask you a few more questions. You don't have to come with us, but it'd be a lot easier on us all if you did."

The color drained from Montgomery's face as he realized he didn't have much of a choice. He slowly stood up and shuffled out of his lab with the two detectives.

Chapter Nine

Joel Williams was looking forward to this evening. Laura was out of town at a two-day workshop on language rights for non-native speakers of English, so Joel was planning to spend the evening catching up with his former boss, Bert Schneider. Williams and Schneider had remained friends after Williams had left the police force, and they got together occasionally for an evening of unhealthy food, beer, and whatever sport was being televised.

Now, as he finished previewing an online video he wanted to show his class the next day, Williams glanced at his watch. It was five-thirty, which meant that if he left now, he'd have plenty of time to stop at home and walk and feed Oscar before heading out to meet Schneider at The Goalpost, their favorite sports bar. He shut down his computer, packed his soft-sided briefcase, and left his office, scooping his navy-blue club jacket off its hook as he went out. Since he hadn't taken the time to pick up his mail that day, Williams decided to stop by the main departmental office on his way out of Carlton Hall. When he got there, he saw Ed Beaumont, the Department Chair, talking

with Shirley Mizzello, one of Williams'
departmental colleagues.

"…just couldn't believe it!" Shirley was
saying.

"Are you sure? Jesse Montgomery?" Ed
asked.

"Of course I'm sure. I served with him on
the Grants and Funding Committee for two
years. I know who it was."

"What's going on?" Joel asked.

"Oh, hi, Joel," Ed stepped back to include
Joel in the conversation. "Shirley was just
telling me she thinks one of the Music
Department's people has been arrested or
something."

"What?" Joel asked. "What are you talking
about? What happened?"

"OK, here's what I saw," Shirley said, with
her usual directness. "I was walking back
here after a meeting over at the
Administration Building. I was passing by
Lessner Hall, and I saw Jesse Montgomery
walking out of it with these two guys. They
put him in the back of what looked like a
city car."

"So you think these guys were cops?" Joel
asked

"Well, they weren't uniforms. It was the
way they put Jesse into the back of the car –
it sure looked like procedure, if you know
what I mean." Shirley had spent years as an

attorney and then Superior Court judge before entering the teaching profession. She was thoroughly familiar with police procedure.

"Well," said Ed, "whatever's going on, I'm sure it'll get around. It's strange, though. I haven't worked with Jesse that much, but I know him slightly. It's weird when someone you know gets arrested."

"He's in the Department of Music, you said?" Joel asked.

"Yeah," Shirley said. "I don't know him really well, but I think he does the Music Theory classes. Why, you know him?"

"No, just wondering. Anyway, I'd better get out of here, or I'll end up staying until midnight. You know how it is."

"I sure do. See you, Joel."

Williams waved a goodbye, stuffed his mail into his briefcase, and left the office.

Once in his Dodge sedan, Williams began to think about what Shirley had said. First that music student had died, and now one of the faculty over there had been arrested. Something was going on over there, and Williams couldn't help thinking the two events might be connected. This made him think again of the conversations he'd had with Patricia Stanley. She'd been pretty sure that her partner hadn't died by accident and hadn't committed suicide. For a kid of nineteen who didn't have some kind of disease, that left just murder. Patricia hadn't mentioned Jesse Montgomery, but who knew? Williams had learned that you never really knew everything about anyone, even your partner. Maybe Montgomery was connected with Serena Brinkman's death. Now he was more eager than ever to get together with Bert Schneider.

By this time, Williams had arrived at his house. He parked the car in the driveway, got out and walked back down the driveway to the mailbox. Then he returned to the house and unlocked the front door, where Oscar greeted him with his usual enthusiasm.

"Hiya, boy! Ready to go?" Williams asked as he leashed Oscar up. Oscar's happy barking was response enough. The two of them took their usual early-evening walk through Williams' neighborhood and then, when they'd returned to the house, Williams filled Oscar's food bowl and replenished his water. "OK, I'm going out for a while. No ordering Chinese food while I'm gone!" he jokingly told Oscar. Then, after a quick check of the house to be sure all was well, Williams left to meet Bert Schneider.

The Goalpost was locally known for its two huge flat-screen televisions, its specially-seasoned chicken wings and its old-fashioned personal service. Most of the staff knew the regular patrons by name, and some even remembered what patrons liked to eat and drink. When Williams got there, he was greeted by co-owner Marty Warner.

"Hey, Joel! Been awhile! How are you?"

"Good, thanks, Marty. Just busy. Bert here yet?"

"Not yet, but I'll have someone bring you a beer while you wait."

"That'd be great – thanks."

Within minutes, Williams had gotten his beer, ordered a plate of chicken wings, and was sitting in a booth.

About ten minutes later, just after the chicken wings had arrived, Schneider joined him.

"Hey, Bert, how are you?"

"Sorry I'm late. Had a last-minute mess to clean up before I left. You know how it is."

"Yeah, I do. Hope it's under control now."

"I think it is."

"Good." Williams took a pull of his beer, and then said, "We had a little mess of our own over at Tilton today."

"That right?"

"Yeah. I heard one of the people in the Department of Music went off with a couple of your guys."

"Yeah, well…." Schneider thought for a moment. Then he picked up a chicken wing and slowly said, "We were looking for some stolen property and we found it."

Williams thought about what Patricia Stanley had told him earlier. Then he took another sip of beer, chose a chicken wing for himself and said, "I guess if anyone might know about a missing violin, someone in a music department would know."

Schneider looked up quickly. "Yeah, I guess so," he said. Then, when Williams didn't add anything, he said, "You know anything about that?"

"You know what campuses are like. People saw a professor being led away by cops. Talk gets around."

"I mean about the violin."

Williams was silent for another long minute. Then he said, "One of my students lost her partner last week. Girl called Serena Brinkman. Seems she died of a severe allergic reaction to peanut flour. My student says this girl was in the music department, that she was a talented musician – played the violin. She said that violin was valuable."

"Who is this student?"

"Her name's Stanley – Patricia Stanley."

"Stanley? I think my guys talked to her."

"They might have. She said she talked to the police."

"Your student say anything else?"

"I don't need to tell you how to do your job, Bert."

"No, but if you've got something, I'm interested."

"Well, Patricia says her friend died of a severe allergic reaction, probably to peanut flour."

Schneider nodded, "Go on."

"She also said Serena wouldn't have eaten anything with peanut flour in it on purpose. She knew about her allergy, and she was too careful for it to be an accident. No reason for suicide, either."

"If it's the same girl, she said the same thing to my guys."

Williams paused a moment as he thought about how best to put the next point he wanted to make. Then, he said, "Bert, Patricia isn't irrational and she's not a drama queen. If she says there's something wrong about her friend's death, it's because she really thinks so."

Schneider took a thoughtful sip of his beer. Then he said, "My guys – Logan and Foster are working this one – didn't get the impression she's irrational or a liar. Maybe a little too eager, like kids can be. They watch too much cop TV."

Williams smiled and said, "Yeah, you wouldn't believe the number of students I have who start out thinking you can solve a murder in an hour."

"Wish it was that easy."

For a few moments, the two men ate in comfortable silence. Williams knew there were limits, even for an ex-cop, to what Schneider could tell him. Still, Williams had to admit he was curious about what Logan and Foster had found. Besides, if Patricia's information was useful, he wanted to be sure that Schneider got it. So he decided not to drop the subject of Serena Brinkman's death just yet. After taking another sip of his beer, he said, "I'm no expert, but the way I've always heard it, people with severe allergies carry injectors with them. If I had that kind of allergy and I were having an allergic reaction, first thing I'd do would be to use the injector."

"Yeah, if the injector's full. If it's been emptied, you're out of luck."

"Guess you are. And you find an empty injector, you want to know why someone has it."

"That's what my guys are wondering, too."

"Told you I didn't need to tell you how to do your job. You want something valuable badly enough, like an expensive violin, you'll do what it takes to get it."

"Exactly."

Again the two men lapsed into silence as they finished their meal. It sounded to Williams as though Schneider and his team were doing their jobs; he'd expected that. Still, it was good to hear. For his part, Schneider respected Williams' way of thinking about things. He knew, too, that Williams knew a lot about what went on at Tilton; he knew that girl, Patricia Stanley, too. So he said, "Your student have anything else to say?"

"Well, I told her if you have a murder, you have to have a murderer. Then I asked her if she knew of anybody who might have wanted her friend dead. She had a couple of ideas."

Schneider looked up, interested, and said, "That right? What'd she say?"

"She mentioned the violin, but you know about that."

"Yeah, that's what Foster and Logan are looking at now. We think we've got something there."

"She also said there was a guy who was interested in her partner. Didn't want to take 'no' for an answer. She said his name's Tony Ferguson."

"Yeah, Foster mentioned that name. Anything else?"

"Well, this Serena Brinkman was rich. Money's always something to think about."

"Got that right."

"She'd just won a competition, too. From what I know, those things can make or break a music career."

"They matter a lot, that's for sure."

Schneider drained his glass and said, "Guess I'd better go before it gets too late. I'm not twenty-five anymore."

"Yeah, me, either," Williams said ruefully. The two men straightened up and Williams left a tip on the table. Then, after paying at the register for their meal, they said a quick goodbye and headed for their separate cars. Each felt that he'd gotten some good ideas from the other; that was part of why they kept in touch.

Jesse Montgomery was also at a restaurant that night. At the moment, he was sitting across the table from his lawyer at a burger place two blocks from the Tilton police station.

"It was humiliating!" Montgomery said. "They took my fingerprints! They even took a mug shot! I've never even had an overdue library book before."

"Look, you were lucky it wasn't worse than it was. For now, they just have theft charges against you. That's what they're going to bring up at your preliminary hearing."

"What do you mean, 'for now?'"

"Don't you realize? They're considering murder charges against you."

"Murder? I didn't kill Serena Brinkman. I didn't even know she'd died at first. And I certainly didn't know she was allergic to anything. I even tried to tell the police that, but they wouldn't listen."

"Jesse, they found an empty auto-injector in her violin's accessory case. You had the violin. You even admitted you were going to keep it. On the face of it, it looks like you did kill her."

"You think I killed her, too?"

"No, frankly, I don't. But you're going to have to tell me everything if you expect me to convince anyone else of that. I can't help you if you hold anything back."

"I'm not holding anything back! Like I told you and those pig-headed, officious policemen, I never even opened the accessory case. I had the violin. I admit that. I was even going to keep it. That was stupid, I admit it, but I couldn't resist. Perhaps I'm guilty of theft, although frankly, I don't think so. After all, Serena gave the violin to me. But I'm not a murderer."

"OK, if I'm going to help you, I need to know everything that happened that day."

"Well, I'd asked Serena for her violin so I could include it in my study. She brought it to me after her competition – that was on the day she died. Then we went to the reception. That took place right after she won."

"Did you see her after the reception?"

"No, the last time I saw her was just after I gave her a glass of champagne to celebrate."

"You gave her champagne?"

"Well, yes, but – wait! You think I poisoned her champagne?"

"Look at it from the police's perspective, Jesse. You wanted the Amati and you took it. You gave that girl champagne. She died a few hours later from a severe allergic reaction. What are they supposed to think?"

"But I didn't kill her! I didn't! I told you, I didn't even know she had any allergies. In fact, I barely knew her at all. What am I going to do?"

"Well, I'll do the best I can for you. You know that. But I'll have to be honest, it doesn't look good. Unless there's some other way that injector turned up in Serena's violin case, it sure looks like you put it there."

Montgomery stared miserably at his practically untasted food. Until that moment, he hadn't realized the seriousness of his situation. Now he felt his comfortable life crumbling around him. His lawyer looked at him sympathetically and said, "Look, I'm going to do all that I can for you. I've known you a long time, Jesse, and I just don't think you'd lose your head and kill someone like that. But it's not going to be easy. You just hang in there and I'll see you at your hearing tomorrow afternoon." Montgomery nodded dully and stood up. He absently shook his lawyer's hand, stopped at the cash register to pay the tab, and then stumbled out into the misty night.

Marcie Bratton was also feeling miserable that night. Ever since Tessa Oliver and then Patricia Stanley had returned to campus, she's felt more and more convinced that Serena must have told them her secret. She must have. Now, Marcie lay on her bed, wondering what she ought to do about it. So far, her C.O. hadn't said anything to her, but that was just a matter of time. Marcie knew what campus gossip was like. The minute there was a good story, it went around campus instantly. The thing to do was to find out what Tessa and Patricia knew. There was just a chance that Serena hadn't said anything to them. Before panicking too much, Marcie would have to find out what those girls knew. She decided to start with Tessa, since she was still in Marcie's building, although she was now on a different floor. That decision made, Marcie sat up, pulled a t-shirt on over her tank top and sweat pants, and went down two floors to Tessa's room.

Tessa had been focusing as much as she could on her schoolwork. It helped her to have something to do and besides, she'd let her work slide while she was at home. Now, she welcomed the distraction of catching up. She was working through some problem sets for her Calculus II class when she was interrupted by a knock on the door.
"It's not locked," she called out.
The door opened and Marcie Bratton came in. "Hey, Tessa, how's it going?" she asked.
"OK, I guess. How are you doing?"
"OK. I just wanted to check and see how you were holding up."
"Thanks. I'm OK. Work helps," Tessa said, pointing at her book.
"Good. Hey, you got a minute?"
"Sure, what's up?"
"Well, it's about Serena. Did she tell you anything about me before – before she died?"
"About you? No. Why?"
"You're sure? She didn't say anything?"

"Marcie, what are you talking about?"

"Nothing. I just wondered. People spread gossip, and I hate that. I just wondered if Serena did."

"If Serena did what?" said a voice behind them. Marcie turned and saw Patricia framed in the doorway.

"Oh, hi, Patricia. What are you doing here?"

"Well, I stopped over to say, 'hi' to Tessa. We got to talking and it got late, so we decided I'd crash for the night. So what's this about Serena?"

"Well, I was just wondering if she said anything to you about me."

"Not to me."

"Me, either," said Tessa.

"You guys aren't lying, are you?"

"Marcie, what's going on? Why would Serena say anything about you? I thought you two got along," Patricia said.

"Nothing's going on. I just don't like gossip, and I wanted to be sure she wasn't spreading any gossip about me."

Tessa said, "Well, stop worrying, OK? She wasn't a gossip. You know that."

"Well, just remember not to believe anything she told you about me. And if you hear anything, just ignore it."

"OK, whatever," said Patricia.

Marcie didn't want to risk getting the girls angry – at least not now. So she said, "OK, then," and was soon gone.

After she'd left, Patricia said, "Do you have any idea what that was about?"

"No clue. You?"

"Nope. It was weird, though."

"Yeah, I wonder what she was talking about."

At ten o'clock that night, Spencer Brinkman was sitting with Natalie, his brother Cole, Cole's wife Elaine and their son, Troy at Pauline's, an upscale restaurant about halfway between the two families' homes. At first, Natalie hadn't wanted to go out, but finally decided that it was better than staying at home with the ghost of Serena's presence still in the house. Besides, she liked Cole and Elaine, and Troy had always been a friend of Serena's as well as her cousin. During the meal, the Brinkmans talked about the rainy weather, Troy's upcoming semester break, their jobs, in fact, just about everything but Serena. It was as if by mutual consent, they'd agreed to avoid talking about the loss they were suffering. They'd finished their dessert, paid the bill and were sipping their coffee when Cole gently said, "Spencer, I hate to bring this up, but we need to talk to Fred Prescott." Fred Prescott had been the accountant for both Brinkman families for fifteen years.

"What do you mean?"

"Well, we need to have Fred go over Serena's accounts."

"I guess you're right," Spencer said slowly. "We need her accounts audited before – well, before her estate is settled."

At the mention of the word, "estate," Natalie gripped her husband's arm, and Elaine looked down at her empty coffee cup. Troy stared straight ahead.

"If you want," Cole went on, "I can give Fred a call. It'll save you the trouble."

"Thanks, Cole, but I'll do it. I should, anyway."

"All right. I'm sorry I had to mention it, but, well, it has to be done."

"No, you right, it does have to be done. I'm glad you reminded me."

At that, Spencer swallowed the last of his coffee. Then he said, "It's getting late and we all have a drive. Let's get going."

The two families gathered their things and prepared to leave the restaurant. After promising to be in touch soon, they went to their separate cars and settled in for the drive home. Once in their Range Rover, Elaine said to Cole, "I'm glad you brought that up to Spencer, Cole. I wouldn't have wanted to."

"Well, I felt bad doing it, but I just didn't see a choice."

"No, I think you did the right thing, don't you, Troy?"

Elaine glanced in the rearview mirror at her son. Then she said, "Troy, what's wrong? You look terrible. Are you all right?"

"I'm all right," he mumbled. "This whole thing with Serena's death is just hard, that's all."

"Of course it is. We're all hurting."

"And now you're talking about her money like she wasn't even a person! Why can't you just leave it alone?"

"Honey, we have to go through her accounts. It's part of settling her estate. I know it sounds cold, but it really does need to be done."

"No, it doesn't! At least not now. Can't it wait?"

"Why are you so upset about this?"

"I don't know. It just seems, well, cold."

"I know it might seem that way, Troy, but it really is the best thing."

Troy didn't answer. He just shook his head and stared out the car's window at the falling rain.

Elaine glanced at him once again, started to say something, and then stopped. Troy must really be feeling Serena's death. No wonder he reacted so strongly against their talking about her money. Well, he'd always been fond of Serena, so that wasn't surprising. Elaine would have to remember to be a little more sensitive when she discussed Serena. Poor Troy.

Chapter Ten

Joel Williams took a quick walk around his house the next morning looking for anything he might have left lying around, with Oscar happily trotting after him. Williams wanted the house cleaned up before Laura got back that evening. He wasn't a sloppy person as a rule, but he knew his wife would be tired and wouldn't want to be confronted with a mess, so he was extra careful to pick up after himself today. When he was satisfied that the house was clean, he leashed Oscar up and took the cheerful mutt for a walk around the block. When they got back to the house, he checked to be sure that Oscar had food and water and told him, "I'll be back this afternoon." Then he petted Oscar, grabbed his briefcase, a blazer and his car keys and locked up the house.

As he pulled his car out of the garage, Williams felt glad that yesterday's rain had stopped. The sky was still a sullen, dreary gray, but at least the drive to work would be easier. He pressed the garage door control in his car and waited until the door had completely shut. Then he pulled out of his driveway and headed towards campus. When he got there, he was a little annoyed to find that there were no parking spaces anywhere near Carlton Hall. With an irritated sigh, he circled campus until he finally found a space in a parking lot near the Administration building a few blocks away. Williams got out of his sedan and after checking to be sure he hadn't forgotten anything, locked the car and walked towards Carlton Hall. His route took him past Lessner Hall and at the sight of the music building, Williams glanced at his watch and decided he could spare some time to walk through it.

Once he'd entered the building, Williams crossed the lobby and, on an impulse, followed the signs that directed him towards the recital hall. His conversations with Patricia Stanley and Bert Schneider had convinced him that Serena Brinkman had been murdered, and now, although he'd never even met this girl, he was curious about it. One of the reasons he'd gotten into law enforcement was that he was irresistibly attracted to puzzles and mysteries, and this certainly was one. Maybe someone in the music department could tell him something about Serena that would help him.

When Williams got to the recital hall, he pulled open the double doors and entered. There was nobody in the auditorium but

Williams' curiosity drove him through the hushed dimness down the main aisle towards a small staircase that led to the stage and in a moment, had entered the small backstage room where performers waited. He walked back to the stage and then returned backstage where he noticed a door leading out of the backstage room. He was on the point of opening the door when it pushed open from the other direction, startling him for a moment.

"Sorry to startle you," said the man who'd pushed open the door.

"Not a problem."

"Are you faculty here?"

"Well, not here. I'm Joel Williams, from Criminal Justice."

"Joel Williams? Did you by chance use to be a cop?"

"Yeah, I was."

"Wondered if you were the same guy. I'm Alex Logan, Tilton PD. Captain Schneider's mentioned your name a couple of times. So have some of the guys who've been in the department for a while. They said you were on the force and then turned professor."

"That's me. Nice to meet you," Williams said, putting out his hand for a shake. "How long have you been in the department?"

"I've been in Tilton for five years. Before that I was a detective up in Reading."

"Bit different here."

"Yeah, but the work's still the same. I still don't get to see my wife very often."

"Now you know why I'm not in the department any more."

The two men laughed for a moment. Then, Williams said, "Mind if I ask what brings you here?"

"We're doing a homicide investigation."

Williams paused a moment, choosing his words carefully. Then he said, "Heard a kid from this department died last week. That kind of thing gets around a campus."

"Guess it does."

"It's a damned shame when kids die young. I heard this kid had talent, too. A violin major."

Logan, sensing an opportunity to learn more about Serena, asked, "You know her?"

"No. I know her partner, though. Patricia Stanley. Nice girl – a crim. major. One of my advisees."

"That right? My partner talked to her, actually."

"She's got her head on straight."

"Seems like it."

Williams was glad to get Logan's hint that the police were taking Patricia seriously now. He looked again around the backstage area and then offered a hint of his own. "I think the musicians wait back here to perform, don't they?"

"That's what I hear."

"If that door's unlocked, anybody could come in and somebody on stage wouldn't know."

"If the room's empty, yeah. Nobody'd see you."

"You leave something like a backpack or instrument case here, and anything could happen to it."

"Good point," Logan agreed.

"Well, listen, I'll let you get back to it. Don't want to get in the way."

"Nice to meet you."

"You, too." The two men shook hands and Williams left the backstage room through the door that Logan had used. He soon turned a corner and found himself back in front of the main entrance to the recital hall.

After he passed the recital hall, Williams continued down the corridor towards the main office for the Department of Music. He stepped in and saw that nobody was sitting at the reception desk. Another quick glance at his watch reassured Williams that he still had a little time, so he decided to wait a moment to see if the receptionist would be back. As he waited, he noticed a large sign labeled "Fall Schedule" on the wall to the left of the reception desk. More to occupy himself than anything else, he wandered over and looked at the schedule of classes being offered that semester. His eye was caught by Jesse Montgomery's name. As he recalled, that was the professor who'd been accused of stealing that Amati. He was idly speculating on what would happen to those students when the receptionist, who'd been in the ladies' room, returned.

"May I help you?" she asked.

Adopting his most affable smile, Williams said, "Yes, thanks. I'm wondering if you have a list of fall events. I see the class schedule here, but not the events."

"Oh, sure. Here's a list if you want to see it. We usually post this on the wall, but I've been making some changes to some of the dates and I didn't have it done yet."

"Thanks. I appreciate it."

The receptionist watched curiously as Williams scanned the list. When he'd found what he wanted, he said, "Thanks again. Now these competitions are usually in the recital hall, right?"

"Yes, that's right. Did you want to take a tour or schedule something? Or are you a parent?"

"Oh, no, thanks. I'm a faculty member from another department. I lost my calendar of events, and thought I'd stop by."

"Oh, well, if you want, I can put one in the interoffice mail for you as soon as I get this revised."

"Great, thanks."

Williams left his name and office location with the receptionist and then took his leave.

After he'd left the main office, Williams checked his watch and realized that he was going to have to head over to Carlton Hall if he was to have time to check his messages and read his mail before his Juvenile Justice class. As he left Lessner Hall, he began to process what he'd learned from his short visit there. Serena Brinkman had been in the recital hall at Lessner shortly before two o'clock the day she died, and she'd waited in the backstage room until it was her turn to perform. Presumably, she'd brought her violin case with her and would have left it backstage while she was performing. If she had, that meant that anyone who knew she would be there could have tampered with her auto-injector, if she'd left it in her case. From what Schneider had hinted, Williams guessed that Serena had put her auto-injector in the violin case. Besides, it made sense that someone with allergies as severe as Serena's would have an auto-injector close at hand. If the police had found that injector empty, as Schneider's comments had suggested, it could be that Montgomery had been responsible for Serena's murder. It seemed clear to Williams that they police thought so and on the surface, it looked that way. There was only one problem with that line of thought: according to the schedule of fall classes, Montgomery had been teaching from one to three o'clock that day. Unless Montgomery had gotten access to Serena's violin case earlier in the day, Williams didn't see how Montgomery would have been able to tamper with that auto-injector.

That realization caused Williams to turn sharply and head back into the building. He was hoping that Logan might still be there, so that he could mention his idea to the detective. Logan wasn't in the recital hall when Williams returned to it. That meant Williams would either have to walk around looking for him or ask for him at the receptionist's desk. Neither was an attractive alternative, since Williams didn't want to be late for class, and didn't want to pique the receptionist's interest more than necessary. In the end, he chose what he saw as the lesser of two evils, and headed towards the receptionist's office.
He was just about to enter when he saw Logan further down the hall, walking with what looked like a student. They went into a

room on the left, and Williams followed them there.

When he got to the room, Williams saw that the door was partially open, so he tapped gently on it and said, "Sorry to interrupt." Logan and the student, a young Asian woman, looked up. Logan said, "Sorry, I'll be back in a minute," to the woman and came to the door.

"What's up?" he asked in a low voice.

Joel drew him outside and said, "I didn't realize you were talking to someone – sorry about that. I'm on my way to teach or I'd have waited. Look, this is a little awkward. I don't want to tell you how to do your job. But if you didn't get a chance to check the fall schedule of classes, you might want to."

Logan raised his eyebrows a little. Normally, he'd have been annoyed at this interruption, but he'd heard Joel Williams had been a good cop. Besides, he was a good cop himself; any useful leads were worth hearing about.

"OK, I will. Thanks."

Williams nodded, apologized again and quickly left. Logan would take it from there.

When Williams had gone, Logan returned to the small conference table where he and

Michelle Park had been sitting. He glanced down at the notepad he'd brought with him and said, "I'm sorry about that, Ms. Park."

"That's OK."

"I just want to ask you a few questions about Serena Brinkman."

"Well, I can't say I knew her very well. We weren't friends. I'll do my best, though."

"You had classes with her, right?"

"Yes, we were both violin performance majors."

"And you both competed for the…Young Artists' Orchestra?"

"That's right."

"How did you get along?"

"Like I said, we weren't friends."

"Enemies?"

"No, of course not. Rivals is more like it."

"Did you know that Serena was allergic to peanuts?"

Michelle thought for a moment. "Yes, Serena told me about it one day."

Logan nodded and said, "This competition you were in – Serena won it, didn't she?"

"Yes, she played very well that day."

"And you came in second?"

"Yes."

"So now you've taken her spot. Is that right?"

"Well, yes."

"You must be very excited about the orchestra and the tour."

"I am. It's an honor."

"Means a big career boost, too, doesn't it?"

"I suppose so, yes."

"Did you see Serena the day of the competition? I mean, before the event?"

"Only for about five minutes. We waited backstage together."

"Did anyone come in or out of the backstage room while you were there?"

"Just Ben Lessner. He was the other competitor. First he played, then Serena played, then I played."

"Then what happened?"

"Well, then we all went onstage and they announced that Serena had won."

"And after that?"

"We went to the reception. I only stayed for a few minutes."

"Did you see Serena eat or drink anything?"

"She had a glass of champagne. I saw it in her hand."

"Anything else?"

"I didn't see her with anything else."

"You give her anything?"

"No, I told you I left the reception early."

Logan looked for a moment at this young woman with the impassive face. Then he said, "Ms. Park, we're trying to find out what happened to Serena. Can you give us any help at all?"

"I'm sorry. I really didn't know her well, and I don't know anyone who'd have wanted to hurt her."

"Not even you?"

"Me? Oh! You mean because of the competition? No, I wasn't out to hurt her. In fact, I respected her. I wanted to win, sure, but not enough to kill her. I didn't even see her that day until we were backstage."

"And you didn't give her anything to eat or drink?"

"No, I told you that."

"You won a big competition because of her death."

"Yes, but there are other competitions. Besides, you don't understand. I didn't hate Serena. I envied her because she played so well, yes. And I wanted to win, of course. But it wasn't personal. It wasn't worth killing for."

Logan realized he wasn't going to get much more out Michelle Park. Not without evidence. So he said, "OK, thanks for what you've told me, Ms. Park. Please stay on campus in case there's anything else we want to ask you."

"Of course."

Michelle left the room as Logan made some notes on his memo pad.

While Logan had been at Lessner Hall, Dan Foster had been talking to Serena Brinkman's parents again. He hadn't found anything that made him seriously suspect either Spencer or Natalie Brinkman of murder, but you always focused on the family first in this kind of investigation. You never knew what might be going on between parents and their children, especially with big money involved. Now he sat with the Brinkmans in their living room, making notes as they talked. Fortunately, they understood that he had a job to do and they didn't seem to mind answering his questions.

"So your daughter had access to this trust fund?" Foster asked.

"Limited access, yes," Spencer Brinkman replied. "She would have gotten full access when she turned twenty-one."

"Anyone else have access?"

"No. The way the trust fund was set up, Serena got access to the trust fund twice a year for an amount equaling college tuition and books. Nobody else could touch it."

"You set this fund up for her?"

"No, her grandfather did. He had a fund set up for her and one for our nephew, her cousin Troy."

"Same terms for both funds?"

"Yes."

Foster wasn't looking forward to his next question. "You folks didn't have access?"

"What are you suggesting?" Natalie Brinkman snapped. Spencer touched his wife gently and said, "He has to ask these questions, Natalie." Slowly, Natalie nodded and said, "I'm sorry. I overreacted. It's just – if you knew how much we loved Serena. She was everything to us. That anyone would imagine we would kill her, well, it's monstrous."

"Nobody's accusing anyone of anything, Ma'am," Foster said. "I can understand your resentment, but the fact is, your husband's right. We have to ask all kinds of uncomfortable questions."

"I know. I'm sorry. Go on."

Spencer returned to the topic at hand. "You were asking us about access. We didn't have any access to Serena's trust fund. My brother – Troy's father – and I had had a falling out with our father. It got ugly and he cut us out of the financial loop."

Foster nodded in comprehension. There went a major motive. Well, he hadn't liked the Brinkmans for this murder, anyway. You had to check, though.

"OK, anyone else in your family we should talk to?"

"You mean people Serena was close to?"
Natalie asked.

"Exactly."

"Well, she and Troy were close. I think they talked all the time, and I know they visited each other."

"Thanks." Foster noted Troy's name on his memo pad. He and Logan had seen that name on Serena's cell phone contact list. He'd pay Troy a visit.

After thanking the Brinkmans for their time, Foster finished his visit and left Devon. He would follow up on Troy Brinkman.

Joel Williams had just finished with his Juvenile Justice class. He was pleased with the way the class had gone that day. He'd had his students prepare a debate on trying juveniles as adults, and he'd been very happy with the results. It always made for a more interesting class if students got involved themselves, instead of just listening to a lecture, and Williams included student activities and input in his class sessions whenever he could. He glanced at the teacher's desk in the classroom to be sure he hadn't left anything there, and then returned to his office. A quick check of his Email revealed nothing urgent, so Williams decided it was a good time to take a lunch break. He gathered up his briefcase and today's edition of the campus newspaper. Then, picking up his jacket from its hook, he left his office and made his way towards the Kozy Korner Kafe.

When he got to the Kozy Korner, Williams saw that it was closed. A large hand-lettered sign on the door said, "The Kozy Korner Kafe is closed today due to flooding in our storeroom. We apologize for any inconvenience." With a muttered epithet, Williams turned around and made his way to the Pit Stop. He didn't like the Pit Stop nearly as much as he liked the Kozy Korner, but today he'd have to put up with it. When he got to the Pit Stop, Williams joined the line of lunchtime customers. He chose a pre-packaged roast beef and cheese sandwich, an apple and a cup of coffee, and then, after paying for his purchase, took a seat. He shook open his paper, took a sip of coffee and began to read.

A moment later, Williams had almost forgotten about his food. The newspaper had devoted an entire page to Serena Brinkman and her death, and Williams read the article eagerly. When he was finished, he pushed the paper aside and began to eat and drink, his thoughts entirely taken up by his

[233]

curiosity about Serena's death. Williams had a habit of getting curious like that; it was part of what had made him a good cop, and he gave into it now. Serena had lived in Cooper Hall, right on campus. That meant that she probably spent most of her time on campus. If that was true, then anything she ate or drank would probably have come from campus. It wasn't a sure thing, of course, but it made sense. Of course, there was no telling whether anyone would remember having seen her the day she died, but Williams couldn't help wondering if anyone had. He finished his coffee, bused his table and then folded his newspaper back to reveal the article he'd been reading. Then, he rejoined the finally dwindling line of customers and chose a candy bar. When it was his turn to pay, he put the newspaper on the counter so he could reach for his wallet. Then, noticing that the cashier was looking at the paper, he said, "Shame about that student."

"Yeah, pretty sad."

"You know her?"

"Oh, no. I just saw her here sometimes. She came in a couple of times a week."

"Yeah?"

"Yeah, she had her violin with her a lot."

Williams knew his next question was tricky, but he couldn't resist. "Was she here the day she died? Last Wednesday?"

The cashier thought for a moment. "Lemme think. I worked breakfast all last week. Did I see her? Yeah, I did. It was that day, too. I remember because I had to work two shifts on Wednesday. Somebody called in sick and I had to stay through lunch. That's when I saw her."

"Good memory."

"Yeah, well, she was pretty."

Williams grinned. Then he said, "She with anyone or she usually come in alone?"

"Well, that day she was with a guy."

"Yeah?"

"Yeah, dark-haired guy. "

Williams didn't want to call a lot of attention to his questions, so he said, "Guess she had a boyfriend. Anyway, it sure is a shame."

"Yeah, it is."

Williams thanked the cashier, put a tip in the tip jar and then left the Pit Stop. He walked back to his office, deep in thought. Serena had been with someone at the Pit Stop the day she died. It could mean absolutely nothing, but Williams knew that the more the police knew about what Serena did on the day she died, and with whom, the better able they'd be to find out how she was poisoned. So he decided that, thin as it was, he'd pass this lead on to Bert Schneider and his team.

As soon as Williams returned to his office, he closed his door, picked up his phone and called the Tilton police department. He was lucky; Bert Schneider picked up as soon as Williams had been put through to his extension. He told Schneider what he'd found out at the Pit Stop, ending with, "I know it's not much, Bert, but if it helps…."
"Hey, I never look a gift tip in the mouth."
"Hope it's useful."
"We'll follow it up and see where it goes."

"I'm sorry," Ben Lessner said, "I didn't really know Serena very well. I mean, we took some classes together, but that was it."
"You were one of the competitors for the Young Artists' Orchestra, right?" Logan asked. He'd finished writing his notes on his interview with Michelle Park. Now it was Lessner's turn.
"Yes. I knew I wasn't going to win. Michelle and Serena were both too good. But I wanted to get some experience."
"So tell me how the competition worked that day."

"Well, we were all backstage in the recital hall. Then I played, then Serena played, and then Michelle played."

"So when one of you was playing, what did the others do?"

"Waited backstage."

"Did anybody have anything to eat or drink?"

"No, you're not supposed to have food or drink back there. Besides, we were all too nervous to eat. We ate later, at the reception."

"OK, let's talk about what happened after the competition"

"Well, we all went onstage to hear the judges' announcement. Serena won, but you know that. Then, like I said, we went to the reception."

"Did you notice anything unusual about Serena? Did she seem sick?"

"No, not really. I mean, she said she had some stomach acid, but Michelle gave her an antacid and then we all left for the reception. She seemed OK after she took the antacid."

"Got it. Anything else you can think of? I'm just trying to get as clear a picture as I can of what happened that day."

"I'm sorry," Ben repeated, "I can't really think of anything. I didn't even see Serena until it was time for the competition, and even then, I didn't see her for more than a few minutes."

Logan thanked Ben, and then made some more notes on his notepad.

Troy Brinkman was just logging on to his favorite internet gambling site when he heard a knock at his door. He had no idea whom it might be, since only his parents knew he'd come back to Millworth earlier that day. He had just decided to pretend he wasn't in and turn his attention back to the computer screen when he heard another, more insistent knock. This time he shut his laptop, went to the door and opened it. A tall, middle-aged African-American man was on the other side of it.

"Yes?" Troy asked.

"Hi, I'm Detective Dan Foster, Tilton Police Department. Are you Troy Brinkman?"

"Yeah, I am. What's this about?"

"It's about your cousin, Serena Brinkman. Do you have a few minutes?"

Troy motioned Foster inside and then sat down slowly on his desk chair. "Yeah, I guess so." He'd figured this would be coming, but Foster's visit still surprised him. Foster took a seat on the room's other desk chair. "Thanks. I understand you two were friends as well as cousins, right?"

"We hung out together sometimes, yeah."

"When was the last time you saw her?"

"Well, I spent Harvest Day weekend with her. That was the weekend before she died."

"Not after that?"

"No. The next thing I heard, she'd died."

"So you didn't see her the day she died?"

"No, I didn't."

"Did you know any of Serena's friends on campus?"

"Well, I know Patricia – Patricia Stanley. That's her partner. There's Tessa Oliver, too – her roommate. I didn't know anybody else she hung around with."

"OK, anything else you can tell me? We'd really appreciate any help you can give us to find out what happened to your cousin."

"I'm sorry. I can't. I mean, we were friends, but we went to different schools. I didn't see her that often. So….you don't think this was some kind of accident? I mean, it doesn't make sense that anyone would murder Serena. Everybody liked her. It must have been an accident."

"We're keeping all the possibilities open. It doesn't really look accidental, though."

"So you think it's murder?"

"Like I said, we're trying to keep all possibilities open. That's why we're asking questions. Are you sure there's nothing else you can tell me?"

"No, I'm sorry."

"OK, thanks. Can I reach you here if there's anything else I need to ask you?"

"Uh, yeah, sure."

When the conversation was finished, Foster made a few notes, and then thanked Troy for his time. After he'd left, Troy pulled his laptop open again and, as it started up, stared blankly at the screen for a few minutes. So the police thought it was murder. The detective hadn't exactly said so, but the message was clear. Troy let the conversation sink in as he thought about what that would mean.

While Troy had been talking with Foster, Tony Ferguson had been talking with Foster's partner, Logan. Tony had been in his room working on some of his other profiles for his "People to Watch" article when Logan had stopped by. Now, Logan was sitting on Tony's bed, making notes on his memo pad.

"So you were doing a profile on Serena Brinkman?"

"Yes. She was one of my "People to Watch." I'm doing this article for the *Vintage* about rising stars on campus and she was one of them. I didn't know her really well, though."

"I've heard you liked her."

"She was nice, yeah."

"You ask her out?"

"Yeah, maybe. Why?"

"We're just trying to find out what happened to her. The more you can help us, the better."

"Look, she said, 'no,' OK? Not one of my best moments."

"I heard you didn't let it go."

"What do you mean?"

"Well, I heard you came around a lot. Asked her out more than once, that kind of thing."

"So I tried again. I didn't hurt her or anything."

"Must have made you pretty mad, getting shot down like that."

"Happens to all of us. Hey, wait! You think *I* had something to do with Serena's death?"

"Did you?" Logan wasn't afraid of being direct.

"Of course not. I couldn't even get close to her. She lied to everybody about me, so they all thought I was out to get her. It was her fault."

"So you didn't see her the day she died."

"No, I stopped by. I was going to give her flowers, but that idiot of an RA of hers made a huge scene. If you really want to investigate Serena's death, you should talk to her."

"Who? The RA?"

"Yeah. If you ask me, she hated me because she wanted Serena for herself if you know what I mean."

Logan made a note to find out who Serena's RA had been, and talk to her.

Chapter Eleven

By six o'clock that evening, Joel Williams was more than ready to leave his office. After his conversation with Bert Schneider, he'd had two committee meetings, both of which had lasted at half an hour longer than they'd been scheduled. That meant he hadn't had any time between meetings to get anything else done, so he'd had to stay at the office almost an hour longer than he'd intended. He'd finally finished organizing his papers and was just about to leave his office when Patricia Stanley appeared in his doorway.

"Hi, Professor Williams. You got a minute?"

"Sure, Patricia. Come on in."

"Oh, it won't take that long, and I can see you're about to leave. Sorry about that."

"Not a problem. Shoot."

"Well, Natalie and Spencer Brinkman – Serena's parents – are going to be in Tilton tomorrow. They're setting up a memorial fund in Serena's name, and they're coming in tomorrow to sign the papers and get their pictures taken and all that. Then they're taking me to dinner, and I want them to meet you, too. We're going to the Grill House at six-thirty. Can you and Mrs. Williams come?"

"Thanks, Patricia. It sounds like a nice evening. I'll check to make sure we don't have anything else going on and then let you know, OK?"

"OK, that'd be great. I'll stop by in the morning right before class."

"Sounds good. See you then."

"OK, see you."

With that, Patricia was gone. Williams was pleased with the invitation to meet Serena's parents; he hadn't been able to shake his interest in Serena's death, and he was hoping that he might learn more about her. Besides, he and Laura both liked the Grill House, which was one of Tilton's mainstays. The Grill House had served the best steaks in town and elegant gourmet stuffed potatoes for decades, and was the top choice of visiting parents who wanted to take their children out for a special treat.

Detective Alex Logan glanced at his watch. It was just before six, and, so he'd been told, a good time to find Marcie Bratton in her dorm room. After his meeting with Tony Ferguson, Logan had gone to the office of the Dean of Students and found out the name of Serena Brinkman's RA. A few questions there and a telephone conversation with Tessa Oliver had helped him learn Marcie's schedule and given him a little background on her. He tapped on her door and opened it when he heard a muffled, "C'mon in."

"Hi, are you Marcie Brinkman?"

"Yes, I am. Can I help you?" The slim, athletic-looking young woman with the strawberry-blonde hair looked at Logan with some confusion.

"I'm Detective Alex Logan, with the Tilton PD."

"Oh," Marcie's brow cleared. "You're here about Serena Brinkman, aren't you? My Residence Director said somebody might come by and want to talk to me, since I was her RA."

"That's right. I do have a few questions for you if you don't mind."

"Sure. I mean, I didn't know Serena all that well, but if I can help…"

"Thanks. We're just trying to find out what happened to her, and anything you can tell me will be helpful."

"I'm not sure I can really tell you that much."

"Did Serena have any arguments with anyone on the floor? Like her roommate?"

"Tessa? No, she and Serena got along just fine."

"How about Serena's partner? Any fights?"

"No, not that I knew about."

"Anybody else have a problem with her?"

"No, that's the strange thing. That's why I think it must have been some kind of accident."

"What about you?"

"Me? What do you mean?"

"Did you get along with Serena?"

"Of course I did. I liked her. She was a nice kid."

"No trouble between you?"

"No, of course not. Why would there be?" Logan paused for a minute. Then, as was his custom, he plunged right in. "She had a partner. If you were interested, too, that might cause trouble."

"Me? You think I was interested in Serena?"

"That's what I heard."

"That's ridiculous. Who told you that?"

"Were you?"

"No, I wasn't. Listen, Detective Logan, there's a lot of gossip around here. There are people here who'll say anything if someone will listen."

"People do gossip," Logan said, to keep the conversation going. Then he made a note to himself on the memo pad he carried with him and glanced around Marcie's room. Noticing a uniform draped over Marcie's chair, he said, "Oh, you're in ROTC?"

"Yeah, this is my third year."

"So you're planning a military career?"

"That's right. I'd really like an Army career and besides, they have great scholarships and other help. It really makes it easier to pay for school."

"Wouldn't be easy to have an Army career if you're gay, would it?"

"What! Me? Gay? Who told you I'm gay?" Quick to realize he'd upset Marcie, Logan said, "Look, your personal life is your business. I'm just trying to find out what happened to Serena Brinkman. Nothing you say needs to go further than this room, but I need to know anything that might have something to do with her death. If you were interested in her and she turned you down…"

"I don't know who you've been talking to, but I *wasn't* interested in Serena! She lived on my floor and I thought she was a nice kid and had talent. That's all."

Logan realized he wasn't going to get a lot more out of this line of questioning, so he switched topics.

"You knew she had a competition last week, right?"

Marcie realized she would have to be careful, so in a calmer voice, she said, "Sure, yeah, everybody on the floor knew that."

"You see her that day?"

Marcie laughed for a moment. "Yeah, I saw her that morning. She'd fallen asleep on the couch in the lounge and I had to wake her up."

"I'll bet that embarrassed her."

"Yeah, it did. She was almost late for class. Didn't even have time for breakfast."

"You usually eat breakfast together?"

"No, but I saw how she was rushing around. She was in such I hurry I decided to be nice and give her a bagel and some coffee."

"That was nice of you. She seem OK then?"

"Yeah, she seemed nervous, but fine. It was a big day for her."

"You make it to her competition?"

"No, I had drills with my brigade that afternoon."

Logan continued to make notes on his memo pad. When he was finished, he said, "Well, I appreciate your time. If you think of anything else…"

"Of course."

After he'd locked his office and collected his mail at the main departmental office, Williams walked back to his car. He got in and headed home after a quick stop at an ATM machine and a local wine shop where he picked up a bottle of chardonnay. When he got home, he put the wine in the refrigerator, then quickly walked and fed Oscar. He and the dog had just gotten back to the house when he heard Laura's Mazda pull into the garage. With a smile, he headed to the kitchen and pulled out two wine glasses. Then, he heard Laura call out, "I'm home!"

"In the kitchen," he called back.

Laura left her suitcase in the living room for the moment and followed her husband's voice into the kitchen, where he was just pouring out the chardonnay.

"How nice! Thank you!" Laura said as she accepted the glass Joel held out to her.

The two of them carried their glasses into the living room where Joel sat down on the sofa and then patted the seat beside him. "I want to hear about the conference," he said.

Laura took him at his word and told him about the workshops she'd attended and the speakers she'd heard. Williams wasn't on the police force any more, but he still liked to keep up with what was going on in the D.A.'s office. Besides, the more information he had, the more he could share with his students. So he listened attentively as his wife told him what she'd learned.

When Laura was finished, she said, "So what's new around here?"

"Well, if you're up to it, we have a dinner invitation tomorrow night."

"Oh? Who invited us?"

"Well, you remember that student – the violin major – that died last week?"

"You mean that student that was your advisee's partner?"

"Yeah. Turns out her parents are in town tomorrow, and they're taking Patricia Stanley – my advisee – to the Grill House. They want us to meet them at six-thirty."

"That'll be really nice. I like the Grill House. Oh, speaking of dinners, how'd your dinner with Bert go?"

"Oh, we always like the Goalpost. We had an interesting conversation, too."

"Don't tell me, let me guess. You talked about that student's death, right?"

"Maybe," Joel grinned at his wife. Then, with a more serious expression, he said, "Bert and his team think this was a murder."

"So your advisee was right?"

"Looks that way."

"OK, so who'd want to kill her?"

"The way I see it, there are a few people who could have wanted her dead. She'd just won an important competition. That's a big deal in the music department, from what I hear, and she had a rival. Could be the rival."

"Well, that sounds logical, anyway."

"Yeah, but she was also seen that day with somebody else – a guy. Wouldn't have been a boyfriend, but it seems there was this guy stalking her. If she said, "no," once too often, well, that might set a kid like that off. Then there's the money."

"There was money?"

"Oh, yeah, there's lots of money in the family. If her death means a lot of money to someone, that would do it, too."

"Wait a minute," Laura said. "Wouldn't somebody with an allergy like that have an auto-injector?"

"Yeah," Joel responded. He thought for a minute, then said, "And they found this kid's auto-injector in her violin case, empty. If she'd used it herself, she probably wouldn't have died. And somebody with that kind of allergy would have noticed if her auto-injector was empty before she put it in the case. So whoever killed her probably tampered with the auto-injector while the case was backstage at the performance."

"She could have left the case somewhere else earlier in the day."

"Possibly, but I don't think so. This was a really rare violin – an Amati. She wouldn't just leave its case lying around. And besides, she'd have had the auto-injector with her, except when she was onstage."

Laura sat quietly for a moment, processing what Joel had said. Then she said, "So whoever did this was probably…"

"…at the performance. Exactly! *And* gave her something with peanut flour in it. Thank you!"

"For what?"

"You always help me organize my thinking." Joel smiled at his wife; he really did depend on her clear, logical thinking, and this time was no exception. He started to say more about the case, but thought better of it. He wanted to do some more thinking. Besides, he'd missed Laura, and he could always call Bert Schneider later…

It was two o'clock in the morning, and Marcie Bratton had never felt less sleepy. She'd been lying awake for hours trying to figure out what to do. It was obvious that somebody had told the police about her. It couldn't have been Serena, so it had to have been Tessa or Patricia – or somebody one of them had told. Marcie couldn't believe anyone would be that cruel; she was going to lose her chance at the only career she'd ever really wanted. Her eyes filled with tears as she thought about it. Then, angrily, she tried again to decide what she ought to do. There was just a chance that whoever told the police hadn't told anyone else. As far as Marcie knew, the only people who might have talked to the police were Patricia and Tessa. Maybe they hadn't told anyone else, although Marcie highly doubted that. Still, she should definitely find out which of them had opened her mouth. Then she would take care it from there. It wouldn't be a good idea to make a scene at this hour, so Marcie decided that she'd deal with those girls in the morning. Satisfied that she wasn't going to be able to do anything else for now, Marcie closed her eyes and finally drifted off into a fitful sleep.

At seven-thirty the next morning, Alex Logan and Dan Foster were having a cup of coffee at The Alarm Clock, a café across the street from the police station. Neither of them had gotten a lot of sleep the night before, and they said little as they sipped their drinks. Finally, Logan took a bite of the toasted bagel he'd ordered and after another drink from his cup said, "So what do we have on the Brinkman case?"

"The way it looks," Foster responded, "we've got a few people who could have wanted that girl dead. What we need to do is figure out who's on that list who was also at her performance."

"And who gave her something with peanut flour in it."

"Exactly."

Logan pulled out the small memo pad he'd been using for his notes. He scanned it briefly, then said, "Looks like the guy we really liked for this is out of it. Turns out he was teaching at the time. I checked, too – he was in class. He stole the violin, but he didn't go backstage. He couldn't have done this."

"So he didn't see the kid earlier in the day? Maybe have a chance then?"

"Nope. I've been following up on what she did that morning. Nobody puts her over at Lessner Hall until just before the performance. And nobody puts Montgomery anywhere but Lessner Hall."

"So do we know who was at the performance?"

"Lemme see… OK, Michelle Park – that's the rival. She was there. She could have done it, but it's hard to see how, with the other performer there backstage. It's possible though. She gave Serena an antacid, too. Could have had peanut flour on it."

"Maybe. And then there's the cousin – Troy Brinkman. He says he wasn't at the performance, and he goes to school an hour away. Still, I found out that he inherits a lot of money now. They both have trust funds that are set up so that if one dies, the other gets it all."

"There's the RA, too."

"The RA?"

"Yeah. I talked to her last night. I don't have anything definite, but I think she might be hiding something."

"Most people do. Any idea what it is?"

"Just an idea. She's in ROTC – wants a military career. If anything got in the way of that, well, it might be worth killing for."

"Depends what got in the way."

"Exactly. When I was talking to Tony Ferguson – that's the photographer – he said the RA might have been interested in Serena."

"…and if that's true, she's got two reasons to want Serena out of the way."

"Yup. She wouldn't want the ROTC folks to know she's gay and if she was interested in Serena, and Serena turned her down, that could cause trouble."

"Yeah, but did she go to the competition?"

"That's the thing. I don't think she was there. She was scheduled for drills with her brigade that afternoon. I have a call in to her CO. If she was there, I don't see where she'd have time to empty the auto-injector."

"What about that photographer?"

"I checked up on him before I left campus yesterday. He was doing an interview for some article he's writing and shooting. I still gotta check and see if he could've had time to run over to Lessner."

Foster glanced at his watch. "It's almost eight. Captain Schneider should be there by now. Let's fill him in and then we can look at some of these people more closely."

"Yeah, we should go."

The two men pushed back their chairs and, after leaving a tip in the tip jar, left The Alarm Clock and headed across the street to check in with their boss.

At eight-fifteen that morning, Tessa Oliver was checking her appearance in the mirror over her dresser before leaving for breakfast and her first class. She combed through her hair once more, and then picked up her backpack and slipped her student ID and cell phone into the pocket of her jeans. She had her hand on her door to open it when a hard knock on the other side startled her. She caught her breath and then opened the door. Marcie Bratton was waiting for her.

"Oh, hi, Marcie. What's up?"

"I'll tell you what's up, you bitch! You told the police."

"What are you talking about?"

"You know what I mean. How could you?"

"How could I what? Why don't you come in and tell me what you're talking about?"

"Don't you dare try to suck up to me! You've ruined me!"

[256]

"What do you mean?"

Marcie stepped closer to Tessa and angrily hissed "Don't pretend you don't know. You and your big mouth have just robbed me of any chance I had at a military career. I am going to get even with you!"

With that, Marcie whirled around and stalked away. A frightened Tessa stepped back into her room and sat down slowly on her bed.

While Tessa had been getting ready to leave, Michelle Park was just arriving at the FreshNow grocery store to start her work shift. She didn't mind working in the early morning; in fact, she preferred it to working later in the day since the FreshNow tended to be more crowded in the afternoons and evenings than it was before lunch. She went into the store and, after hanging up her coat, clocked in at the machine located in the short corridor between the storeroom and the employees' lounge. Then, she put on the FreshNow apron and name pin she'd brought with her and headed towards the front of the store to find her boss and get her instructions for the day. Within a few minutes, she'd established herself at one of the cash registers.

She hadn't been at her station for more than fifteen minutes when a customer whose order she was about to ring up asked her a question.

"I'm looking for peanut flour," he said, "and I couldn't find any in your baking aisle. I looked in your organics aisle and in produce, too, and didn't find it."

"Oh, I'm sorry. We don't sell peanut flour here."

"OK. Do you know where I might be able to get some?"

"Gosh, I don't know. Maybe a specialty store or online?"

"OK, thanks."

With that, Michelle's customer placed a box of cereal and a can of tomato sauce on the conveyer belt and, when she'd rung up his order, thanked her again and paid. She handed him his change and the plastic bag in which she'd placed his items. Then the customer left and Michelle turned to wait on the next person in line.

On his way out of the FreshNow, Joel Williams thought carefully. As soon as he'd come into the store, he'd recognized the young lady at the register as the woman that Alex Logan had been talking to in the music building yesterday – the same girl who'd won the musical competition after Serena

Brinkman had died, he guessed. Otherwise, why would Logan have been interviewing her? If she had poisoned Serena, she'd have had to get the peanut flour from somewhere. Clearly not where she worked, but it had been worth asking about. It didn't sound like she was familiar with where to buy peanut flour, either, but you never knew. In the meantime, he was going to be late for a meeting he'd scheduled with Ed Beaumont if he didn't move quickly.

That thought was enough to hurry Williams to his car. He tossed his groceries in the back seat and, as fast as he safely could, drove to campus. He was lucky enough this morning to find a decent parking place, so getting into Carlton Hall didn't take as long as he'd been afraid it might. He grabbed his briefcase, got out of the car and, after locking it, headed towards his office building. After grabbing his mail and saying a quick, "Hello," to Noelle Sanders, the department secretary, Williams went to his office to leave his briefcase and gather what he would need for his meeting. When he got to the door of his office, he saw Patricia Stanley waiting for him.

"'Morning, Patricia," he said as he unlocked his door. "What's up?"

"Hi, Dr. Williams. I just wanted to stop by and see whether you can meet us at the Grill House tonight."

"Oh, yes, thanks for reminding me about that. We'll be there. Six-thirty, right?"

"Right."

"OK, and thanks for the invite."

Patricia smiled and, seeing that Williams seemed to be in a hurry, said goodbye and headed off to class.

Williams quickly picked up what he'd need for his meeting and then went down the hall to Beaumont's office. Fortunately, this would be an easy meeting; Beaumont just wanted to go over some changes to the department's course offerings for the spring semester. He arrived at the open door to the Chair's office and tapped on the doorframe. Beaumont looked up from his computer screen.

"Oh, hi, Joel, come on in."

"Thanks." Williams took a seat at a small table in the corner of Beaumont's office. In a moment, Beaumont had joined him there.

"Thanks for coming in," Beaumont began. "I wanted to get your input on what we're offering for the spring and when before I finalize the schedule. They need it next week."

"Got it."

With that, the two men settled down to work. Williams felt lucky that there weren't going to be any new courses offered this spring, so he only needed to pay cursory attention to the tentative schedule. He couldn't stop thinking about Serena Brinkman's murder and the pieces of information about it that he was slowly gathering. There were some moments when he really missed being a part of the detective force, especially when he was slogging through schedules, paperwork, and the other administrative parts of his job. After about half an hour, he and Beaumont had finished going over the plan, and Williams prepared to go back to his office and get ready for his Law Enforcement Procedures class.

"Thanks, Joel, I should have the final copy of this to everybody by Monday, so you can all sign off."

"That works for me."

With that, Williams returned to his office and glanced at his watch. There was just enough time for a quick internet search he wanted to do. He turned on his computer and, while it was booting up, looked over his lesson plan notes and gathered some student papers he planned to return. When the computer was ready, he began his search.

That girl at the FreshNow had suggested he check specialty stores for peanut flour, and Williams had decided to find out whether there were any stores like that in the Tilton area. He couldn't think of any, but then, he and Laura didn't go to that kind of store very often. Williams wasn't an internet expert, but before long, he'd found three gourmet specialty food stores within fifty miles of Tilton. Of course, it was possible that someone had ordered peanut flour online, but there was no way for Williams to check that; he was sure the Tilton police would follow up on that, anyway. It was also possible for somebody to have bought it at a store that was farther away from Tilton than fifty miles. But he doubted that, especially if the killer was a student. Williams wrote down the names and addresses of the stores, closed out his internet window, and then got ready to go to class.

"Just a minute," said the manager of the Pit Stop. "I have to check the schedule and see who was working that day." Alex Logan had gone there to follow up on something Bert Schneider had told him and Dan Foster during their morning meeting. Someone who worked at the Pit Stop had seen Serena Brinkman eating lunch with a guy the day she was murdered. Of course, there were any number of dark-haired guys on the Tilton campus; there was nothing to say which one of them it might have been. But it was a major break to have pinned down a place where she'd been seen eating something with someone. Finally, the manager looked up in triumph. "Here it is. Adam Graves was working that day."

"Thanks. Is he on duty right now?"

"No. He's not scheduled until five. He works dinner tonight. You want his number?"

"That'd be great."

Logan took down the number and, after thanking the manager, left the tiny back room of the restaurant and went out into the large main lounge of the Student Union Building. There, he pulled his cell phone out of his pocket and punched in the number he'd just been given. Fortunately, Adam Graves was in his dorm room. Fifteen minutes later, Logan had arrived at the right building and found the room number he'd been given.

He knocked at the door, and a second later, a tall, thin student with sandy hair and a straggling attempt at a moustache opened it.

"Are you Adam Graves?"

"Yeah, that's me."

"I'm Detective Alex Logan, Tilton PD. We talked a few minutes ago."

"Oh, yeah, come on in," Graves said. He was almost excited at being involved in a police investigation; it was just like a TV show.

"Thanks." Logan went in and perched on the end of Logan's bed; it was the only surface in the room not strewn with papers, clothes and books. When he'd settled himself, he said, "Like I said on the phone, I want to talk to you about this girl – Serena Brinkman."

He showed Graves a photo of Serena.

"Oh, yeah, her. There was another guy asking about her just yesterday."

"That right? Who was he?"

"Dunno. Some older white guy – kinda gray hair. Tall, no beard, no moustache."

Logan smiled to himself; Schneider had told him and Foster about Williams' phone call.

"Got it." Then, hoping to refocus Graves on the matter at hand, Logan asked, "So, about this girl – Serena Brinkman. You saw her the day she died?"

"Yeah," Graves responded, relishing the chance to be important. "She was with this guy, and they were having lunch."

"You remember what he looked liked?"

"Dark haired dude – white guy."

"He one of these guys?" Logan pulled out two photographs and showed them to Graves.

"That looks like him," Graves said. He pointed to a picture of Troy Brinkman.

"You sure?"

"Well, I couldn't go to court, but it looks like him"

"Thanks," said Logan. "That's real helpful."

"Are you gonna put that guy in a lineup or something?" Graves asked with almost ghoulish interest.

"Right now, we're just asking questions," Logan responded. He'd dealt with curious witnesses before, and he knew the kinds of wrong ideas people got when they watched cop shows too often.

"Oh, well, you gonna arrest him?"

"Like I said, we're just asking questions, and you've been really cooperative. I appreciate it."

Graves finally got the hint. Somewhat reluctantly he said, "Yeah, no problem."

Logan made some notes to himself, and then, after thanking Graves once more, left his room. He had another lead to follow, and now was as good a time as any to do it. He headed over to Lessner Hall and, after asking around a little, tracked down Michelle Park, who was just finishing a practice session. He knocked on the door of the practice room she was using and, when she opened it, said, "Glad I found you, Ms. Park. I've got a few more questions for you."

Michelle swallowed hard, then said, "Uh, sure."

Logan sat down on a chair, and Michelle took a seat on the piano bench that was the only other seat in the practice room.

"Is this going to take long? I have to finish practicing, and then I have class and then orchestra practice."

"Sounds like you're a busy person."

"Yeah, I guess so."

"You have a job, too?"

"I work at the FreshNow. Why?"

"Just sounds like you have a lot going on. Lot of stress."

"I guess so."

"Especially with you being a musician."

"Look, what are you getting at?"

"You and Serena Brinkman were in an important competition. Somebody under a lot of stress might do anything to win."

"Are you accusing me of killing Serena?"

Michelle hadn't said much, but she was certainly following Logan's logic.

"I'm wondering why you didn't tell me about the antacid you gave Serena right after the competition."

"Antacid?" All of a sudden, the color drained from Michelle's face.

Logan, quick to notice her reaction, said, "Serena said she had some stomach acid, and you gave her an antacid tablet. Isn't that right?"

After a pause, Michelle said, "Yes, but -"

"So why didn't you tell me about that before?"

"Because I forgot. It was such a little thing. I just didn't think about it, and besides, it wasn't really food or drink. I thought that's what you meant."

"It would have been enough to kill Serena."

Michelle's face crumpled. She swallowed hard again, and then said, "Look, Detective. I wanted to win that competition. I really did. But I didn't kill Serena."

"You wanted her out of the way."

"You don't understand at all!" Michelle was practically in tears now. "Yes, the competition was important. It meant everything to me. But I didn't want Serena dead. She made me play better. I wanted to beat her, not kill her."

Logan nodded slowly as he made notes on his ever-present memo pad. "How important was it to beat her?" he asked.

"I didn't kill her," Michelle said.

"But you were jealous of her, weren't you?"

"A little. Who wouldn't be? She had money. She had talent. She had everything. But I didn't hate her. I just wanted to win."

"How badly?"

Michelle looked away for a long moment. Then, her face once more expressionless, she looked squarely at Logan. "You don't understand how much stress we musicians live under. That competition was the most important thing in the world to me. But I did not want Serena dead, and I did not kill her. You have no evidence that I did. Now, I have to get to class." She drew herself up and, without a backward glance, left the practice room. As soon as she was out of sight, all of the bravado seemed to leave her. She stood leaning against a wall of the corridor for a moment to try to gather her thoughts and recover. How had that detective found out about the antacid tablet? Of course!! Ben Lessner had been backstage that day, too. *He* must have told the police. Well, she couldn't lean against this wall forever. She would have to figure out what to do now. Straightening up, Michelle drew a few deep breaths. Then, her thoughts whirling, she made her way slowly up the two floors to her next class.

Chapter Twelve

Joel Williams was pleased. After his Law Enforcement Procedures class, he'd returned to his office and, happily, hadn't been faced with anything urgent. That left him an hour and a half before a meeting he had scheduled with one of his advisees. Enough time to go over to the police station. Ordinarily, he'd just have called, but he wanted to check on two of the department interns anyway and besides, he owed Bert Schneider a cup of coffee. So he grabbed the piece of paper on which he'd written the names of the specialty stores he'd located. Then, after a quick glance around his office, Williams grabbed his blazer and left his office. He took the stairs to the ground floor of Carlton Hall and in a moment, had reached his car. The traffic was light and the weather was good, so within ten minutes, Williams had arrived at the police precinct. He parked and went into the building.

Once inside, Williams asked at the reception desk if Bert Schneider was in. After asking Williams' name, the receptionist buzzed Schneider's desk and, within moments, Schneider himself came through the door that separated the waiting area from the main part of the police station.

"'Morning, Joel. How are you?"

"Hey, Bert."

The two men shook hands, and then Schneider said, "Something up?"

"Just thought I would stop by and pay up on that cup of coffee I owe you."

"Give me two minutes."

Schneider was as good as his word, and within a short time, the two men were seated across the street at The Alarm Clock. After an experimental sip of his still-too-hot-coffee, Schneider said, "So what's up, Joel?"

"It's about that Serena Brinkman case. I'll be honest, Bert. I don't want to butt in, but I was doing some poking around."

"Oh, yeah?" Schneider raised his eyebrows. "You find out anything I should know about?"

"Maybe. Here's what I've been thinking. Whoever poisoned that girl had to buy peanut flour. I found out it's not that easy to get unless you buy it online. I did some looking, and there's really only three places where somebody local would have bought it."

"I've been kinda thinking the same thing. Find out who bought peanut flour and you find out who might have used it."

"Right." Williams reached into his pocket and pulled out the piece of paper on which

[270]

he'd written the names of the specialty stores he'd located. He slid the paper across the table to Schneider, who took it with a nod of thanks.

"Appreciate it. This'll help my guys."

"Hope so. I hate it when kids die young. I'd like to see you get whoever did this."

"Yeah, so would I."

Williams decided to take a chance. After a moment, he said, "You getting anywhere?"

"Yeah, we are. There's a few people we like for this."

Williams nodded. "That's good," he said. He stopped himself from asking Schneider to be more specific. He knew Schneider couldn't answer him anyway. For a short time, the two men silently sipped their coffee. Then, with a glance at his watch, Williams said, "Guess I'd better get back to the office. I have a meeting in a little while."

"Yeah, I should earn my living, too."

The two men drained their cups, pushed back their chairs and left the café. They crossed the street and parted ways when they got to Williams' car.

When Bert Schneider got back to his office, he found Alex Logan and Dan Foster deep in conversation in a small conference room that was used for meetings and, sometimes, for interviews. He walked in and said, "Sorry to interrupt."

"No problem," Foster said. "What's up?"

"Just wanted to give you guys this."

Schneider pulled the list Williams had given him out of his pocket and tossed it on the conference table."

"What's this?" Logan asked.

"These are specialty stores that sell peanut flour."

Both detectives were quick enough to catch Schneider's meaning.

"We match one of the people we like for this Brinkman case with somebody who bought peanut flour, we got a killer," Foster said.

"Could be," Schneider said.

"We'll check it out," Logan said.

Schneider thanked the two detectives and headed towards his office to plow through the myriad memos and telephone messages waiting for him.

Tessa Oliver looked quickly up and down the hall as she exited the elevator late that afternoon on the way to her dorm room after class. Although she wasn't usually jumpy, she'd been nervous ever since Marcie Bratton's threat that morning. What she couldn't figure out was what had upset Marcie so much. Somehow, Marcie thought

Tessa was responsible for ruining her life, and Tessa had no idea why. She thought about going to the campus police or the Residence Director, but Marcie hadn't really done anything to her. Besides, Marcie was an RA. People wouldn't be likely to believe Tessa over Marcie and even if they did, Tessa had nothing solid to go on. She was just going to have to hope that Marcie would calm down and think more clearly. Until Marcie did something, there wasn't going to be a lot that Tessa could do. In a way, that made it worse. Well, she would just have to do the best she could. With one more glance down the hall, Tessa headed towards her room.

When she got there, she saw that Patricia Stanley was at the door waiting for her.
"Hey, you, what's up?" Tessa asked.
"Remember I left my MP3 player here the other day? I came back to get it."
"Sure, come on in."
Tessa unlocked her door and the two girls went in. Then, Tessa said, "I think it's in my top dresser drawer. I didn't want to leave it out."
Patricia noticed that Tessa seemed nervous, so after she'd retrieved her MP3 player, she said, "Anything wrong?"
"No, I'm OK. Just distracted."

"What's going on?"

"You really want to know?"

"Sure."

"OK." With that, Tessa shut her door and told Patricia about Marcie's behavior that morning. "I really think she's losing it," Tessa said when she'd finished. "I have no idea what she was talking about, but she threatened me."

"You think we should go to the campus police?"

"What am I going to tell them? She hasn't done anything to me, and I have no proof or anything."

"Well, you could at least go to the Dean of Students' office and ask for a room change.

"I might have to, and if I have to, I will. But mostly, I'm worried about Marcie. She used to have it together, you know? But lately, she's been acting really weird."

Patricia nodded thoughtfully. "Yeah," she finally said. "Ever since Serena was killed. Maybe we should go to the Residence Director or something. If Marcie needs help, she should get it."

"I guess so, but I don't know that it'll do any good."

"I think we should, Tessa. Somebody needs to talk to Marcie and straighten her out, or get her some help, or whatever she needs. Besides, if we don't tell the Residence

Director, Marcie could make your life miserable."

"She could make it worse if we do," Tessa said gloomily.

"No. If we report what's going on, you'll be safer."

"Yeah, I guess you're right. Besides, Marcie's obviously going off the deep end. Somebody needs to know about it."

"Come on. I'll walk you down to the Residence Director's office."

"OK," Tessa reluctantly agreed. The two girls got up, left the room and headed down to the first floor of Cooper Hall, where the Residence Director's office was located. When they got there, they saw that Darlene Sheary, the Residence Director, was in. Patricia tapped on the open door and Darlene looked up.

"Come on in," she said. "What can I do you for?"

"You got a minute?" Tessa asked.

"Sure." Then, noticing Tessa's hesitation, Darlene said, "Do we need to talk privately?"

"Well, could I shut the door?"

"OK."

Tessa shut the door and then she and Patricia took seats. Darlene said, "Shoot."

With that, Tessa explained what had happened between her and Marcie. Patricia

[275]

added, "She was acting weird with me, too. Remember, Tessa? She asked both of us not to believe anything Serena told us about her."

"That's right," Tessa nodded.

Darlene waited until both girls had finished. Then she said, "I'm glad you girls came in. And I promise I'll keep your visit confidential. For now, let me talk to Marcie and see what's going on. If anything else happens, let me know. But otherwise, you need to keep this confidential, too, OK?"

Both girls nodded in comprehension. Then, Darlene said, "OK, then. Now don't worry. We'll get this straightened out."

The two girls thanked Darlene for her time and left.

On the way up the elevator towards Tessa's room, Patricia said, "You want me to crash with you tonight?"

"Nah, I'll be OK. I'm glad we went down to Darlene, though."

"You sure?"

"Yeah, I'm sure. Besides, I'm sure you have plans, don't you?"

"Yeah, as a matter of fact. Serena's parents are in town to set up a memorial scholarship fund. They're taking me to dinner at the Grill House."

"That's a nice place."

"You wanna come? I'm sure they wouldn't mind."

"No, I don't want to impose."

"Hey, you were Serena's roommate. I'll bet they would love to see you. Let me call and let them know." At this point, the elevator reached Tessa's floor, and the two girls went out and headed towards Tessa's room.

"You sure?" Tessa asked. But by that time, Patricia had already whipped out her cell phone and found Natalie Brinkman's cell phone number in her electronic address book. Within a minute, she'd gotten through and arranged for Tessa to join the others for dinner.

"That's really nice of you," Tessa said when Patricia had finished her conversation.

"Don't worry about it. It's better than staying here alone. Besides, they are really happy you're coming."

"Well, if I'm going out to dinner, I want to get changed. I look horrible."

"You do not, but OK. How about I meet you at six in the lobby?"

"Got it. And thanks."

Patricia smiled at Tessa and said, "No worries." In a moment, she'd returned to the elevator and was on her way downstairs.

An hour and a quarter later, a freshened-up Tessa Oliver took the elevator downstairs to

Cooper Hall's lobby. She was looking forward to going out to dinner, a luxury she could rarely afford. Besides, she was concerned about Serena's parents; it would be good to see how they were holding up. When she got to the lobby, she saw that Patricia was waiting for her. The two girls greeted each other and left the building. As they left, neither noticed that Marcie Bratton, who'd just left Darlene Sheary's office, was watching them.

The night was a crisp one, so Tessa and Patricia huddled into their jackets as they walked towards Patricia's car. They hopped in and in ten minutes, they'd arrived at the Grill House. After Patricia had parked the car, they went into the restaurant's lobby where the hostess asked for their names and then directed them to where the Brinkmans were already waiting. The Brinkmans greeted Patricia and Tessa warmly, and the four of them sat down. Five minutes later, Joel and Laura Williams were shown to the table.

"Hi, Dr. and Mrs. Williams! I'm so glad you came!" Patricia said. "These are Spencer and Natalie Brinkman. This is Dr. Joel Williams, the professor I told you about, and his wife, Laura Williams. And this is my friend Tessa Oliver. Tessa was Serena's roommate."

Everyone shook hands and murmured greetings. After they were settled, a waiter brought them a set of menus and took their drink orders. Then the group made light conversation as they decided what to order. Laura said, "Patricia tells us that you've set up a scholarship fund."

"That's right," Spencer said. "We wanted to do something in Serena's memory, and, well, this just seemed like a good thing to do."

"I think it's a great idea," Joel said.

Natalie smiled sadly. "Serena always loved playing so much. You should have seen her."

"I wish we had," Laura said.

Patricia said to the Brinkmans, "Did you ever get the chance to look at the video of her performance at the Young Artists' Orchestra competition? She put it on her blog for you."

"We've watched it dozens of times," Spencer admitted. "I'm so glad that you filmed it, since we couldn't be there that day."

"At least she had family there. I'm pretty sure I saw Troy come in."

"Oh, I'm so glad," Natalie said. "He'd called us and told us he was going to surprise her and show up, but that was weeks before the competition, and I wasn't sure he was going to make it."

"Who's Troy?" Joel asked.

"Oh, I'm sorry!" Patricia apologized.

"Troy's Serena's cousin. He goes to school at Millworth – you know where that is? He and Serena were good friends."

"They were," Natalie agreed. Tessa nodded.

At that point, the waiter returned to take their orders. When they'd finished ordering, Spencer returned to the topic of his nephew. "You see," he explained, "Troy and Serena were very close in age. He's a year older. They practically grew up together."

Natalie laughed a moment. "People even used to say they looked like brother and sister. They have the same dark hair and blue eyes."

"They did look a lot alike," Tessa said. Patricia nodded her agreement.

"We don't want to monopolize the conversation," Natalie said politely to Joel. "Patricia tells us you're one of her professors."

"That's right. He used to be a detective, too, and he's helping to find out who killed Serena."

"Oh, are you on the police force?" Spencer asked.

"Oh, no. Not any more," Williams answered.

"Then I don't understand…." began Natalie.

Patricia explained, "Dr. Williams used to be on the police force. Now he's a professor, and my advisor. I asked him to help find out what happened to Serena. He knows a lot of people on campus, and he knows a lot of the police. I figured he could give us useful information."

"So you're working with the police?" Natalie asked.

"Well," Joel answered, "not officially, but we cooperate. They're the ones with the training and the skills, and I'm sure that they'll find out what happened to Serena."

"But you're helping?" Spencer put in.

"Trying to."

"Can you tell us anything? Do you know anything about Serena's death? The two detectives keep telling us they're interviewing people and I know they're working hard, but they can't tell us anything," Spencer said.

"That's because they don't have any definite answers yet," Joel answered. "They'll let you know as soon as they have some solid information. I know it's hard to deal with, but they want to be sure of themselves."

"I guess that makes some sense," Spencer said.

"It's just that it's so hard not to know," Natalie said.

"I know it must be terrible," Joel said, "but the police really are working as hard as they can. I'm sure of it." Then, seeing that the Brinkmans seemed to feel comfortable talking to him, he said, "Is there anything you can think of that would help the police? The more information they have, the better they can do their job."

Natalie said, "We told the detectives everything we could think of. We really can't imagine anyone would want to kill Serena. At first we thought it was the man who stole her violin – did you know about the violin? - but we stopped at the police station this morning on our way into town, and we talked to Detective Foster. He told us that man didn't do it. That was the only reason we could think of that anyone would want to kill her."

Spencer agreed. "Besides," he added, "the police are already interviewing people Serena knew, like her RA, and people she knew in the music department."

"And me, too," Tessa put in.

"It sounds like they're doing everything they can. So am I," Joel reassured them. "We will find out what happened to Serena. And in the meantime, if you think of anything – anything at all – that could help, let the police know right away, or get in touch with me if you're more comfortable doing that."

"All right," Spencer slowly said. He took the business card that Joel had proffered, and tucked it in his walled.

Just then, the food arrived, and everyone began to eat. The meal went more smoothly than it might have, given the circumstances. Although the Brinkmans were distraught about Serena's death, Natalie Brinkman was an accomplished hostess, and her husband had spent years cultivating business relationships over meals. So within a short time, the sense of gloom that had started to settle over the group began to lift slightly.

When the meal was over, everyone gathered purses and coats and prepared to leave. After Tessa and Patricia had thanked their hosts and left the restaurant, Joel and Laura Williams did the same. Then, they headed towards Joel's Dodge. Once they'd settled into the car, Joel said, "You mind if we make a quick stop on the way home?"

"Sure, are we out of something?"

"No. I want to stop at the police station for a minute."

Laura smiled into the darkness. She should have guessed what was on her husband's mind. "Sure, I guess so. I should have figured you'd want to talk to Bert if he's in." Within a few minutes, they'd pulled into the station parking lot. For the second time that day, Joel asked at the reception desk to speak to his former boss. Schneider wasn't there, but Alex Logan was. So Williams asked to speak to him. When Logan appeared, Joel introduced him to Laura. Then, after excusing themselves, they headed back towards Logan's desk.

"Look," Williams said, "I'm sorry to bother you, but I thought you would want to know. My wife and I just had dinner with Natalie and Spencer Brinkman – Serena Brinkman's parents."

"They're nice people."

"They are. Her death has hit them hard."

"I'm sure it has."

"I wouldn't bother you with this, but they mentioned that their nephew – Troy, I think his name is – was a friend of Serena's. I'm sure you've talked to him, right?"

"Yeah, my partner talked to him."

"I figured you would, since he was there that day."

"They said he was there? You mean on campus?"

"Yes, but really I mean at the performance."

"That right?"

"Yeah, that's what they said."

Logan thought for a minute. Then he said,
"Thanks. That helps."

"Hoped it would."

Williams knew Logan wouldn't be able to
say anything more, but he didn't need to
hear anything more, really. He could tell that
Logan didn't know Troy had been there the
day of that competition. Well, if that helped,
then Williams was glad he'd stopped by. He
thanked Logan for his time and left. When
he got back to the waiting room, Laura
looked up from a magazine she'd been
reading.

"All done?" she asked.

"Think so," he said.

When Patricia Stanley and Tessa Oliver got
back to the Tilton campus, Patricia parked
her car and then offered to walk Tessa back
to Cooper Hall. Tessa accepted and the two
girls headed back towards Tessa's dorm
building. They were almost to the building
when Marcie Bratton stepped out of the
shadows and stood in front of them.

"What are you doing here, Marcie? You
scared the hell out of me!" gasped Patricia.

"You're ruining my life, both of you!"

"Marcie, what do you mean?" Tessa said

"You shut up! You're just as bad!"

"Marcie, you need to calm down," Patricia said, recovering slightly. "How did we ruin your life?"

"Like you don't know! You couldn't keep your big mouths shut, either of you!"

"We haven't said anything about you to anyone," Tessa cried.

"Oh, yeah? Then why did I get called into Darlene's office? And why did she ask if I'm in some sort of trouble?"

"Because we're worried about you, OK?" Patricia said. "You've been out of it since Serena died, and we think maybe something is really wrong."

"Well, now you've gotten me into real trouble. Why didn't you just keep your mouths shut?"

"Because you threatened me," Tessa snapped. "What was I supposed to do?"

"That was your own fault! I told you not to believe any gossip you heard, and you went and shot off your mouths anyway! Well, I meant what I said. I don't think you two know who you're dealing with. If you two don't leave me alone and shut the hell up, I will make you regret you came to Tilton. You got that?" Marcie glared angrily at Tessa and Patricia.

Finally Tessa said, "Look, Marcie, whatever we did to upset you, we're sorry. Let's not let this get out of hand, OK?"

Patricia added, "There's no need for a feud."
Marcie drew a breath and then said, "If I see either of you again, or if I hear any garbage you've spread about me, I will make you both pay. And if you don't believe me, just try me!"

Slowly, Patricia and Tessa stepped away from Marcie and began to move towards the dorm building. Marcie called after them, "I mean it!" as they walked off. As soon as they were out of her sight, both girls broke into a run until they got to the door of the building. They got to Tessa's room as soon as they could and, once they were inside, Patricia said, "She's nuts. I really think she's lost it."

"I think so, too."

"You sure you don't want me to crash here tonight?"

"On second thought, you mind?"

"Nah, let me just call my roommate."

Chapter Thirteen

"Are you absolutely sure?" asked Spencer Brinkman.

"Unfortunately, I am," answered Fred Prescott. Since Prescott was the Brinkman's accountant, he and Spencer Brinkman had been reviewing Serena's financial records in preparation for getting her estate settled.

"But that's a twelve thousand dollar difference! What would Serena have needed with that much money?"

"I'm sorry, Spencer, I don't know. The only thing I can tell you is that when we got her trust fund statement from Premier Pennsylvania Bank, this is the balance they gave us. There's one unexplained onsite withdrawal for twelve thousand dollars. That tells me she must have gone into a branch of the bank herself and gotten the money."

"Do you think maybe someone sabotaged her account?"

"Well, I won't say it's absolutely impossible, but they would have checked her ID at the bank before signing over any money, especially an amount like that. So if it was fraud, it was somebody who stole her ID or faked it. I honestly don't think it happened that way."

Spencer sighed, "I guess you're right. I just can't think of any reason Serena would have needed that kind of money without telling us about it. She knew she could always come to us. What about her checking and savings accounts?"

"Nothing unexpected there in the last quarter. There's a transfer from her trust fund – looks like that was used for books. There were online payments for her cell phone, three purchases at some clothing stores, a few smaller withdrawals that were probably pocket money, and one or two restaurant tabs. Nothing you wouldn't expect from a college student. I see a few small deposits to her savings account, but not much there, either."

"So she had money in checking and in savings. Why in the world would she have needed money like that from her trust fund?"

Prescott cleared his throat. "Look, Spencer, it's not my place, but are you sure there was nothing going on that maybe you didn't know about? I mean, Serena was away at school. You never know."

"Fred, I know you mean well, but that's ludicrous. This is a lot of money for us not to know anything about it. Besides, the – the coroner's report said that she wasn't using drugs or anything. We know she didn't have a lot of expensive things with her, so the money wasn't spent on a car or anything. Maybe she gave it to somebody."

"Would Serena really have given a friend that much money without telling you?"

"I wouldn't have thought so, but I can't imagine any other explanation." Spencer didn't know Prescott well enough to consider him a close friend, so he didn't say more. But he was intelligent enough to wonder whether this mysterious withdrawal had anything to do with Serena's death. As soon as he finished with Prescott, he'd get in touch with the police. For now, he and Prescott took a final look at Serena's financial records and then Prescott left after promising to be in touch.

For their part, Alex Logan and Dan Foster were using up department gasoline funds trying to find It's Only Natural, the first of the three specialty food stores on the list Schneider had given them. It was located ten miles outside of Tilton, and getting there had meant a long ride on winding, unmarked rural roads. Finally, out of the corner of his eye, Foster saw a sign. "There it is," he said. "Up there on the left."

"Finally!" Logan responded. They pulled up to the small parking lot in front of the store, got out of their unmarked cruiser and went inside.

"May I help you?" asked a middle-aged woman in an apron who came up to wait on them.

"Yes, thanks," Foster responded. When he and Logan had identified themselves, the woman said, "I'm Dottie Hoffman. I own this store. What's this about? We've never had any trouble with the police before."

"Don't worry, Ma'am," said Logan. "This isn't about you or your store. We're conducting an investigation and we need to ask a few questions, that's all."

"Well, I suppose so," said the owner uncertainly.

"Thank you. We appreciate it. Now, you sell peanut flour, don't you?"

"We sure do. It makes a great lower-fat, high-protein and low-carb substitute in lots of recipes. It's even used in spaghetti sauce."

"That's good to know. You sell a lot of it?"

"Well, I wouldn't say that. We do sell our share, though. People like the high nutritional content."

"Do you keep records of your customers?"

"Oh, my, no. Well, unless they use a credit card. We do have some regular customers, though, that we get to know. What's this about, anyway?" Dottie Hoffman asked with a return to her original suspicious manner.

"We're looking for someone who bought peanut flour within, say, the last three weeks."

"Hm… three weeks. OK. If they used a credit card, I can find it for you."

"Thanks."

A search of the store's records, though, failed to turn up a credit-card sale of peanut flour. "I'm sorry," the woman said, "but the only thing I can tell you is that we've made four sales of peanut flour – each of them a five-pound bag – in the last month. Without credit card information, though, I can't tell you who bought it. Most people pay in cash."

"OK, well, we appreciate your effort. You said you have some regular customers, right?"

"Well, we do have people who come in a lot, yes. Why?"

"Do you recognize any of these people?" Foster held out four pictures. Dottie Hoffman slowly shook her head at the first three photos, but then stopped when she saw one of Marcie Bratton.

"Oh, yes, of course. I know her. I mean, I don't know her name, but I've seen her."

"She shop here a lot?"

"Not really. I've just seen her come in a few times."

"You don't remember if she bought peanut flour?"

"No, I'm sorry. I just know she's been here."

"OK, thanks."

Logan had been busily making notes. Now, after a few more questions, he and Foster thanked the owner for her time and returned to their car. Once they'd gotten in, Foster said, "So, Marcie Bratton's been here. Maybe she bought peanut flour."

"Could be. She had reason to want to shut Serena up, too, if you're right about her."

"Yup. But she was doing drills that afternoon. Her CO says she was there, too. Hard to see how she could have emptied that auto-injector."

"Well, I still think we need to consider her a possible."

"Oh, yeah."

With that, Logan and Foster consulted their list.

"OK, what's next?" Logan asked.

"Place called Mother Earth. It's a drive from here, but it's the next closest place."

"Got it."

The car pulled away from the parking lot.

That same morning, Patricia Stanley sat in her chemistry class, trying to focus on reaction rates. She was a good chemistry student and normally found the class interesting. Today, though, she kept glancing to her right, half-expecting to see Serena sitting there. Patricia knew that dealing with Serena's loss would take her a long time, but it was especially hard when she felt surrounded by reminders of what had happened. Marcie's behavior last night hadn't helped Patricia, either. Fortunately, Patricia had been successful at getting Tessa to tell Darlene Sheary what had happened. Darlene had then gotten approval for Tessa to move to another dorm. It would be annoying for Tessa to have to move her things again, but everyone involved thought it was for the best. Patricia wondered for the hundredth time what Marcie feared so much; she didn't know the RA well, but she'd always thought of Marcie as a calm, rational person. You had to be if you were an RA. Now, though, something had really gotten to Marcie. Idly, Patricia wondered if it had anything to do with Serena's death. After all, if Serena knew a secret about Marcie, that might make Marcie afraid. Fear did strange things to people. Still, Patricia found it very hard to think of Marcie as a killer. But nearly anyone could commit murder if there was enough reason. That brought Patricia back to the question of what Marcie was trying to hide. For the rest of the class, Patricia concentrated only enough to take notes as she thought again and again about Marcie's behavior and what it might have to do with Serena's death.

Logan and Foster had just reached the second of the three specialty stores on their list.

Foster parked the car and the two detectives went up the three steps leading to the front door of Mother Earth, a specialty-foods/organic harvest store. This was a much larger store than the previous store they'd visited. It even had an ATM on the wide porch at the front of the building. Logan and Foster looked around and, after a few moments, found a young woman wearing a brown-and-green apron with the Mother Earth logo on the front.

"Can I help you?" she asked.

"Yeah," Logan answered. "You have peanut flour, right?"

"Sure. We carry dark roast and light roast in 5, 10 and 25-pound bags. What kind are you looking for?"

Logan and Foster showed their police identification. Then, Foster said, "We're wondering if you'd remember or have a way of finding out if someone bought peanut flour recently."

"Like, how recently?"

"Maybe in the last couple of weeks?"

"I'm sorry, but we get a lot of people in here. It's hard to say who buys what. I think we keep credit card records, though. You want me to get my manager?"

"That'd be great. Thanks."

The young woman nodded and moved off. Within a few minutes she'd returned, accompanied by a young man in his early thirties. He had a long dark-brown braid and was wearing a polo shirt with the Mother Earth logo.

"I'm Tim Banks, the store manager. Can I help you?"

"Yeah, thanks," Logan answered. He and Foster again showed their police identification.

"What's going on?"

"We're doing an investigation." Logan answered. He then asked Banks about the store's record-keeping policies. Banks led the detectives to a small office towards the back of the store. "Just a minute," he said, "I'll look at our receipts. This might take some time if you don't have a date to give me."

"Sorry, we don't have an exact date. Just in the past month, if that helps."

"OK, lemme see."

After a few minutes, the manager looked up from his screen. "I'm sorry. I can tell you the number of bags of peanut flour we sold – six. But I don't see any credit card receipts for any of those bags, so I couldn't tell you who bought them."

"Thanks for what you have told us. You mind if we ask your employees a couple of questions?" Foster asked.

"That's fine."

After a little more conversation with the manager, Logan and Foster went back into the main part of the store, where they soon found the young woman who'd greeted them when they arrived. They showed her the photos they'd brought with them, but she shook her head. "I'm sorry, but none of these people looks familiar. We get really busy here sometimes, so I don't remember everybody who comes in. You want me to ask around?"

"Thanks. That'd be helpful," Logan answered. He and Foster accompanied her as she asked the other two employees on duty if they recognized anyone in the photos. Nobody did. Realizing that they'd accomplished as much as they probably could for now, the two detectives thanked their guide and left the store.

On the way out of the store, Logan noticed the ATM. Foster did, too. Their eyes met and Logan said, "Maybe the people who work here don't remember who comes in, but don't those machines take pictures of people who use them?"

"Yeah, they do," Foster said. "It's a long shot, though."

"It is, but it might be worth checking."

"Could be."

When they'd gotten back into the car, Logan noted the store's name and address, as well as the bank name on the ATM.

Deep in thought, Joel Williams hung up his office telephone. He'd just had an unexpected call from Spencer Brinkman, who'd told him about the twelve thousand dollars that was missing from their daughter's account. Williams had suggested that Brinkman tell the police about the money, but Brinkman had told him that neither of the two detectives working on the case was in the office. Williams had promised to pass the information on, and then, satisfied that Brinkman didn't know anything about what had happened to the money, he'd ended the call. Now he sat quietly, sifting through what Brinkman had told him. Like Brinkman, Williams wondered if this money had something to do with Serena's death. Was she being blackmailed? Not likely; blackmailers don't usually kill their victims, and Serena had withdrawn the money, not deposited it. Maybe she'd given the money to someone and then thought better of it. If so, that person must have needed the money badly enough to kill for it. Williams thought a moment longer, then picked up his phone again and within a few moments, had gotten through to Bert Schneider. Schneider would want this information, and so would the two detectives.

Foster and Logan had stopped for a quick lunch at a fast-food restaurant halfway between their second and third stops. Now Foster parked their cruiser at their final stop, the Garden of Eatin'. "Who thinks up these names?" Logan cracked as they got out of the car. Foster shook his head. The two detectives went into the store and, as soon as they'd located a salesperson and identified themselves, asked about peanut flour.
"We do sell peanut flour," said the ponytailed young man who waited on them, "but we have none in right now. We're supposed to get our delivery tomorrow. You could come back then."
"Thanks," Foster said, "We might do that. So you sell a lot of it?"

"Some. It's got a lot of protein and nutrients that wheat and rice flour don't have."

"Would you know if you've sold any in the last month?"

"Lemme check." The young man, who was also the assistant manager, quickly established that three five-pound bags of peanut flour had been sold in the past month. One had been purchased with a credit card. As Logan noted that information, Foster showed the assistant manager the photographs the detectives had been carrying with them.

"I'm sorry, but I don't recognize any of these people. There are some people that come in here a lot, and I know them. But I don't think I've ever seen these people or if I have, I don't remember it."

"We appreciate the help you have given us," Foster responded.

Logan had a few more words with the assistant manager, and then the two detectives left.

Later that afternoon, Joel Williams was in his office grading papers. He wanted to have them done by the end of the day so he could return them to his students at the next class session without having to spend the evening working on them. Like most students,

Williams' students liked knowing how they were doing in class, and frequently mentioned how much they appreciated his prompt feedback when they evaluated his courses. On the other hand, paperwork was not Williams' favorite part of his job, and sometimes it took real effort to stay focused on what he had to do. Finally, Williams gave up and decided he needed a break. He straightened up, picked up his club jacket from its hook, and closed and locked his office. Then, he took the stairs to the ground floor and went outside. It was a crisp, cool afternoon, and the sun was already beginning to lower towards the horizon as Williams made his way towards the Student Union Building for a snack – something more nutritious than vending machine fare.

When he got the Student Union Building, Williams decided he'd get a piece of fruit at the Pit Stop, since the Kozy Korner didn't really sell small snacks. He took his place in line and, after he'd made his purchase, was getting ready to leave when he saw Alex Logan. Unable to resist the temptation to compare notes with the detective, Williams walked over to where Logan was standing. "Hey, how's it going?" he asked.
"Joel, good to see you again."

The two men shook hands. Then Williams asked, "You in a hurry or can I spring for some coffee?"

"I got a little time."

The two men got in line and, once they'd gotten their coffee, headed towards the building's lobby, where it was quieter. They took seats on one of the long, padded benches that lined the lobby.

"So what brings you to campus?" Williams asked, although he'd already guessed what Logan was doing there.

"Just following up on some things."

"You got to be thorough." Then, Williams' curiosity got the better of him. "Hope you're making some progress."

"I think so. It takes some time."

"Yeah, it does. But at least not many places sell peanut flour."

"That's true. All you gotta do is find out who bought it."

"Fortunately, stores and credit card companies keep records."

"Unless people pay in cash."

"Yeah, there's that, of course. But lots of stores have video cameras. They record who buys what."

Logan looked up. He'd been thinking the same thing, and in fact, he and Foster had arranged to get video surveillance tapes from each of the stores they'd visited. "Yup.

You get taped buying something, it's hard to deny."

"Exactly."

Williams then thought of something else.

"Bert tell you I called earlier?"

"Yeah, he did. Thanks."

"Hey, if I can help…."

"In fact, I actually have to get going. Foster and I are heading out in a bit to follow that up."

"Well, I won't keep you then."

By then, the two men had finished their coffee. They stood up and Logan tossed his empty cup into a nearby trash can. Williams asked, "You notice they don't cook?" as he jerked his head in the direction of the Pit Stop's door.

"Yeah," Logan said with a slight smile. It shouldn't have surprised him that Wililams had had the same thought about the food at the Pit Stop, but it did.

"The only food they sell there is packaged and fruit."

"Yup, and you'd think people with allergies would read labels. They wouldn't buy something with peanut flour in it."

"Yeah," Williams said. After a moment's thought, he had an idea. "If you buy something to drink, though, somebody could put something in it."

"Guess so. You get up to use the bathroom or something, somebody could do that."

"My thoughts exactly. Well, lemme let you get back to work."

"Yeah, I gotta go. Thanks for the coffee."

"Not a problem."

After saying goodbye to Logan, Williams headed back towards his office to face the rest of his papers. Laura had a late meeting and wouldn't be home until at least seven-thirty. That would give him some time to try to plow through as many papers as he could. For his part, Logan headed back towards the police station where he would meet up with Foster.

An hour and a half later, Troy Brinkman was sitting slumped on his dorm bed. He had just had a very difficult conversation with his father and he was trying to recover. Cole Brinkman had called Troy with the news about the mysterious disappearance of twelve thousand dollars from Serena's trust fund, and had asked Troy what he knew about it. Troy put his father off as best he could by saying he didn't know anything about it. It was likely enough, after all. But the effort had taken its toll on him. He was just gathering his thoughts when he heard a knock on his door.

"Come in," he called.

The door opened and Troy's stomach churned when he saw the two detectives who'd been investigating Serena's death. Not again!! Doing his best to maintain his composure, he said, "What can I do for you? I thought I answered all of your questions already."

"We just have a few more questions," Foster answered.

"I don't know how much more helpful I can be," Troy answered. "I told you I wasn't at Tilton the day Serena died."

"Well, see, that's the problem," Logan said. "We found out you were there. You even had lunch with Serena."

"Where did you hear that?"

"Someone identified you. Mind telling us why you didn't say anything about that?"

Troy was silent for a moment. Then he said, "OK, I'm sorry. I lied. Serena's death has hit me really hard. I just couldn't deal with being right on campus that day."

"You were at her performance, too."

"OK, you win. I was there. I wanted to cheer her on. Is that so hard to understand?"

"What I don't understand is why you didn't tell us."

"I told you already. I'm just really having a hard time with this. Besides, what if I was there? You think I had something to do with Serena's death?"

"I don't like it when I find out someone's lied to me."

"I had no reason to kill Serena. She was my cousin and we were friends. I liked her. Why would I want to kill her?"

Foster answered that question with another one. "You know anything about a withdrawal from her trust fund for twelve thousand dollars?"

"Yeah, as a matter of fact, my father just called to tell me."

"You know where that money went?"

"No, I'm sorry."

"You sure?"

Now Troy wasn't sure what to say. The last thing he wanted was to antagonize these detectives. Still, he had to say something.

"OK," he finally sighed. "I'll tell you. I think Serena had a gambling problem. Internet gambling."

"What makes you think that?" Logan asked.

"She told me. She said she lost a lot of her own money, and had to take some from her trust fund."

"That would explain the trust fund withdrawal, but you see, there's a problem with that. Serena's accounts didn't show any payments to any online gambling sites. If she were an online gambler, we'd have found that out. You wanna try again?"

"What do you mean?"

"I mean I think you know more about that money than you're telling us."

"You think I had something to do with Serena's death. I keep telling you, though, I didn't kill her. I had no motive. We were friends. Look, Detectives, I don't mean to sound like a snob, but I have plenty of money. My family has money. I wouldn't kill somebody for twelve thousand dollars."

"People have all kinds of reasons for killing other people."

"You really think I killed my own cousin?"

"I don't like it when people lie to me."

"Like I told you, I admit I lied about going to Tilton the day Serena was killed. And yes, I ate with her and I saw her performance. But I did not kill her."

Logan knew they didn't have much to go on yet, but at the same time, he didn't like it that Troy Brinkman hadn't been more forthcoming. He could tell that Foster wasn't happy about it, either. But they were going to need more evidence than a few lies if they were going to take this any further. So, somewhat reluctantly, they got ready to leave. As they left, Foster said, "We'll probably want to talk to you again, so please stay available."

"Of course."

Chapter Fourteen

At eight-thirty the next morning, Joel Williams pulled into the last available parking spot near Carlton Hall. He felt extremely lucky to have found this spot; he'd worked out that morning and his muscles were aching a little. He'd been hoping not to have a long walk to his office. He slowly got of his car and, as he picked up his briefcase, told himself he wouldn't push himself that hard next time he went to the gym. It was not fun to be so rudely reminded that he wasn't twenty-five any more. After he'd stopped in at the main departmental office for his mail and a word of greeting to Noelle Sanders, Williams made his way to his office. He was surprised when he got there to see Alex Logan waiting for him.

"'Morning," Williams said as he unlocked his office door. "What brings you by?"

"Couple of questions. You got a few minutes?"

"Sure. I have class in an hour, but I'm fine for now."

"Good, thanks."

Logan hung his police-issue windbreaker on the hook on Williams' office door and then settled himself into a chair. When he saw that he had Williams' attention, he said,

"What do you think of the Brinkman family?"

Williams' eyebrows went up slightly, but he only answered, "I haven't really gotten to know them that well. They seem nice. They're all broken up about losing their daughter."

"You got a feel for them, though, right? You think there's something going on in that family?"

"I don't think so. Hard to say. You talked to them. What do you think?"

"I think you're right. Here's the thing, though. Their daughter makes a twelve-thousand dollar withdrawal from her trust fund. Mom and Dad have no idea she's done that. Nothing else weird about her money – just normal stuff. Her cousin Troy says she's an internet gambler, but we can't find anything. No credit card payments to gambling sites, no nothing."

"You asked Troy if he knows what happened to that money, right?"

Logan nodded "He says he doesn't know, but Foster and I think he's lying."

"You think maybe he killed Serena?"

"That's the other thing. That's why I'm here. Foster and I were talking this morning, and we're trying to figure out where this kid fits in. I was hoping to get your perspective, since you've talked to the family, too.

Something's going on with him, but he says he had no motive. He liked her. His family's got money, too, so he didn't need that twelve grand. Did her parents say anything about Troy to you?"

"They said the two of them were friends – got along really well. The roommate and Serena's partner say the same thing."

Williams felt himself slipping almost unconsciously into his former detective role as the conversation continued.

"So if they were so close, why do Foster and I think something is wrong?"

"What else did the Brinkman kid say?"

"He said Serena had told him she was an internet gambler, and that's why she took the money from her trust fund. But her accounts came up clean, so it looks like he's lying or she lied to him."

Williams leaned back a little in his chair and half-closed his eyes. After a long moment, he said, "You say they were close, right?"

"Yeah."

"That was the impression I got, too. So they're friends. Friends help each other. What if it wasn't Serena who was in trouble?"

Logan's eyes lit as he absorbed what Williams was saying. "So she gives her cousin the money because he's the one who's the gambler."

"Could be. Ought to be easy to find out."
"But wait a minute. This family's got money. If the kid needed money, wouldn't he just go to his parents?"
"Maybe he did. Once too often."
Logan nodded slowly. "And that family's close. If Serena told his parents he was in trouble and she had to help him…"
"Exactly. Then the kid's out of luck."
Logan nodded again. "Thanks. That fits in."
Williams smiled briefly. "Once a cop, always a cop, I guess."
"Maybe. Anyway, I'd better let you earn your paycheck. I have to get over to the station, anyway."
"Good to see you again, Alex."
Both men stood up. They shook hands and then Logan left. Williams would have liked to go along but, reminding himself that he couldn't, he refocused and turned ruefully back to his desk and the set of journal articles he'd set aside to look over before class.

An hour later, Logan and Foster were sitting in the police station's small conference/interview room. Technicians had brought in a computer, and the two detectives were watching the surveillance films that been sent that morning from the three specialty food stores they'd visited.

They'd started with films from two weeks before Serena Brinkman's murder, and had decided to work their way up to the morning of the murder itself. Fortunately, the department had access to the State Police's new facial recognition software, so Foster and Logan didn't have to watch hours of film; the software they were using would isolate any frames that included people whose photos the detectives had uploaded onto the computer. Within a few moments, the program had flagged three frames from It's Only Natural.

"There she is," Foster said.

"Yeah, but it's hard to see what she has in her hand. Could be a lot of different things." They zoomed the first frame as much as they could. "No good," Logan said. "She's got a bag of cookies."

"Let's keep going. If she buys cookies there, maybe she buys peanut flour, or maybe those cookies have peanut flour in them," Foster said.

Logan agreed, and they checked the other two frames. In those frames, Marcie was buying snacks, but not peanut flour.

"Looks like she's not the one we want." Logan commented.

"Looks like it. You never know, though."

"OK, well for now, let's see what's on those other films."

"Right."

The two men moved on to the film that they'd gotten from Mother Earth. After a short time, Logan said, "Hey, Dan, did you see that?"

"Sure did."

"Bingo."

They watched the rest of the films, just to be sure. It was hard to make a good case if you weren't thorough. Then, they stopped the program and shut down the computer. They left the conference room and headed towards the technology lab to let the tech team know they were finished with the computer. When they got there, one of the technicians said, "Good timing. You guys were the ones who wanted the files from Serena Brinkman's computer, right?"

"Yeah, that's right," Foster said.

"We got 'em for you. Here's the folder with what we found."

"Thanks," Foster said as he took a manila folder from the technician's outstretched hand. "You find anything interesting?"

"We didn't find anything illegal, if that's what you mean. No virus or malware programs, and nothing else really weird. Just documents, Emails, some music recording software, anti-virus software, word processing, spreadsheets, a few games. Otherwise, just the basics."

"Got it. Thanks."

Logan and Foster returned to the conference room so they could spread out the contents of the manila folder and look at it more closely. When they got there, Foster dropped the folder on the table and opened it. He divided the pile of documents in half and pushed one pile of paper across the table. The other he moved closer to himself. Then he said, "Let's go." For a while there was silence as the two men read through the papers. Finally, Foster looked up. "Hey, Alex, look at this." He pushed an Email he'd found across the table. Logan pulled it towards himself and read it. When he was finished, he looked up at his partner. "We might just have what we need here." Foster nodded.

Troy Brinkman pushed the "delete" key of his laptop one last time. Finally, he was finished cleaning up the files he didn't want on his hard drive. He did another search of the files, just to make sure, and then shut down the computer. While the computer completed the shutdown process, Troy tried to think of anything else he ought to do, but couldn't think of anything. What he'd done should be enough. With a slight smile on his face, he packed the notebooks he'd need for his last class of the day into his backpack, and prepared to leave his room. He was just about to go when he heard a knock on his door. He opened the door and almost reflexively stepped back into the room. There were two uniformed police officers waiting for him.

"Troy Brinkman?"

"Yes?"

"You're under arrest for murder."

Troy's face drained of color. One of the officers then informed Troy of his legal rights and handcuffed him.

"But I didn't kill anyone!"

'You'll have to discuss that with your attorney."

The other officer picked up Troy's laptop.

"You can't take that! That's my property!"

"We have a warrant for it, too."

Dazed and silent, Troy was led to the police cruiser and seated in the back. For a time, his thoughts were a blurred and confused. Gradually, though, his mind began to clear. By the time he and the officers had arrived at the Tilton police station, Troy had figured out what he would do. He'd be OK; he would just have to stay calm.

Cole Brinkman got the call at six-thirty that evening. When he finished, he slowly hung up the phone and, with a shaking voice, said to his wife, "That was Troy. He's been arrested for Serena's murder."

"What? But that's impossible!" Elaine cried. "The police must have made some kind of horrible mistake!"

"I think so, too. Troy says it's all a misunderstanding, but I need to go deal with this."

"Of course. I'm coming, too, and we should bring Marv."

"You're right. He might still be in his office. I'll try there first." Within ten minutes, Cole had reached Marv Goldman, the family attorney, and arranged to meet him at the Tilton police station.

Cole and Elaine drove in near silence through the darkness. They were both stunned by the news about Troy, and neither knew what to say. When they got to the Tilton police station, they went inside and were greeted by Marv Goldman, who'd gotten there first. In hushed tones, Goldman explained the procedure for arresting, booking, and scheduling a preliminary hearing. Then, he reassured them, "I'll take care of this whole thing. I'm about to talk with Troy, and then we'll see what the police have to say. I'm sure this will all be straightened out."

[317]

"Can we see Troy?" asked Cole.

"Not right now, but as soon as we're finished with the interview, you can see him."

Just then, the door between the waiting room and the rest of the police station opened, and a uniformed officer walked over to the three of them. "Which one of you is Marv Goldman?" he asked. When Goldman had identified himself, he and the police officer went back through the doors towards the interview room where Troy was waiting.

Cole and Elaine waited for nearly an hour. During that time, they talked little. Elaine flipped through magazines, vainly trying to keep her mind off what was happening. Cole pulled out his PDA, but he was no more successful than his wife was at pushing aside the reality of what was going on. Finally, Marv Goldman returned, accompanied by an officer. Beneath his professional exterior, both Brinkmans could tell that he was upset.

"How did it go, Marv? What's going on? When will Troy be released?"

"I think you both had better come with me." Now more anxious than ever, the Brinkmans rose and followed Goldman and the officer back to the interview room. Troy looked up when he saw them.

"Mom! Dad! Thank God you're here!"

Elaine went over and hugged her son. Cole turned to the two detectives who were sitting across the table from Troy. "Why have you arrested my son? What evidence do you have?"

Logan said, "Troy's under arrest for the murder of his cousin, Serena Brinkman. She died of anaphylactic shock due to exposure to peanut flour. We have evidence that Troy bought peanut flour on the day she died. We have evidence that he had the opportunity to put that peanut flour in her drink, and we have evidence that he could have tampered with her auto-injector."

"But that's ridiculous!" Elaine said sharply. "Troy and Serena were close. Why would he kill her?"

Goldman said, "I think you'd better listen to the rest of what the detectives have to say."

Both Brinkmans turned back to the detectives. Foster said, "We have evidence that Troy's been heavily involved in internet gambling."

"So I gamble a little Lots of people gamble online," Troy protested. "It's no big deal. It doesn't mean I killed anybody."

"We also got copies of Troy's trust fund activity. His account's nearly empty."

Cole turned to his son. "You spent all your money on gambling?" he asked in shocked tones. Then, returning to the more important issue, he asked, "But what does this have to do with Serena's death?"

Logan answered, "We have evidence that Serena probably knew Troy was in trouble."

At this point, Goldman said, "Detectives, I'd like to talk to my clients in private."

Foster and Logan pushed their chairs back and got up. Logan said, "Let us know when you're done." Then the two detectives left the room.

When they'd gone, Cole Brinkman said, "Troy, talk to me. What's going on here?"

Troy looked away and said nothing.

"Troy, what happened?"

Troy still said nothing. He gulped hard, though.

Almost gently, Goldman said, "Troy, I think you'd better talk to your parents."

Troy looked at his parents. Then he looked at Goldman. The reality of his situation was gradually dawning on him, and he was getting more frightened by the minute. With the last of his resistance slipping away, he said, "I didn't want Serena to die. I just didn't have any choice. I was out of money. I asked her for some help, and then she had to go and threaten to tell you."

[320]

"You killed Serena to keep her quiet? I don't believe it! How could you do that?" Cole said in stunned surprise.

Troy watched his parents. As he saw the growing horror on their faces, he felt a surge of self-protection, almost anger. "It's your fault, you know! You were the ones who threatened to take away my money. If you hadn't done that, I wouldn't have had to hurt Serena."

"Hurt her? You *murdered* her!" Cole said, almost in disbelief. Then his face grew harder. He drew himself up and said, "Troy, you killed someone. You murdered your own cousin. And just so we wouldn't find out you were gambling. You disgust me. I don't want anything more to do with you. You'll have to get out of this as best you can. On your own. Come on, Elaine."

Elaine stood up slowly, as though she were in a dream. She was revolted by what it seemed Troy had done, but at the same time, he was her son. She'd never felt so torn in her life.

"Mom?" Troy pleaded. "Aren't you going to help me?"

Elaine drew a long breath. "Troy, you committed murder. What do you expect me to do?"

"Can't you do something to get me out of here?"

"There's nothing to do," Cole answered before his wife could respond. "The police have a lot of evidence. You're going to go to prison for murder."

"I can't believe you're just abandoning me!"

"You brought this on yourself, Troy. Let's go, Elaine." With a final anguished glance at her son, Elaine followed her husband out of the interview room. When they'd left, Troy dropped his head into his hands. He'd been so sure his parents would come to the rescue. After a long time, he lifted his head and saw that Marv Goldman was still in the room. "So what happens now?" he asked the lawyer.

"The detectives will give their evidence to the District Attorney's office. Then they'll decide whether to pursue the case."

"Do you think they will?"

"It doesn't look good, Troy. The D.A.'s office will let me see the evidence they have, and they'll let me know the charges. Then we'll go from there."

"But I'll have to stay here, right?"

"Look, I feel bad for you, Troy, but you were arrested for murder. They're probably not going to release you."

Troy hung his head again miserably.

Chapter Fifteen

Late the next afternoon, Joel Williams was just finishing raking the leaves in his yard. He'd put it off for a few days too long and had finally gotten around to it this afternoon. He bagged the leaves and then went inside to wash up. His hands were still dripping when the phone rang. Annoyed at being interrupted, he dried his hands quickly and barked, "Hello!" into the receiver.

"Sounds like I caught you at a bad time," said Bert Schneider.

"Sorry, Bert. I was in the middle of something when you called."

"You want me to call back?"

"No, that's OK. What's up?"

"Thought you might be interested to know. We got an arrest in that Serena Brinkman case."

"That right? That's good to hear."

"Yeah, thought you'd think so. It'll be in tomorrow's paper, but I thought I'd tell you now."

"Thanks. Hey, if you're not busy tonight, why don't you come on over? We're ordering Chinese."

"Sounds good. I should be done here around seven, so… seven-thirty?

"OK, see you then."

Once he'd hung up the phone, Joel went in search of Laura, who was in their home office. She looked up when Williams came in.

"Honey, you mind if Bert comes over for dinner?"

"No, that'd be nice." Then, a smile of comprehension spread over her face as she said, "They got an arrest in that case you've been following, didn't they?"

Joel smiled back. "That's what Bert said."

Schneider arrived promptly at seven-thirty. After greeting Joel and Laura, he handed Laura the bottle of pinot grigio he'd brought. The three of them settled themselves at the dining room table where they began to open the cartons of Chinese food that Joel had picked up fifteen minutes earlier. As they ate, Joel said, "Glad you got that arrest you were telling me about."

"Yeah, me, too," Schneider said. "That kid died too young."

"You've got good cops working for you. I figured they'd do their jobs."

"Yeah, well, surveillance film tells you who's in a store and what a person buys."

"It does."

"It's pretty amazing, too, what a hard drive will tell you about places people go online."

"That's true enough."

"Yup. You gamble, it shows. You spend too much money doing it, and bank records show that."

"People don't realize how much they leave behind them."

"Good thing, too, or we couldn't do our jobs."

Joel nodded. He might not be able to directly ask about Troy Brinkman's arrest, but at least Bert Schneider had let him know how they'd caught him in his own way. He'd read more about it in the next day's paper.

The next morning, the news of Troy Brinkman's arrest and impending trial was on the front page of the *Tilton Sentinel*. Patricia Stanley read the news as she sipped the coffee she'd made herself. She read the article twice, and then put the paper and her coffee cup down. Her eyes filled with tears for the hundredth time as she thought about Serena. After a long time, she slowly got up and went over to her dresser, where she pulled a tissue from the box she kept there. She blew her nose, wiped her face and returned to the desk where she'd left the paper. She folded it carefully and opened her desk drawer. In the drawer was a photo of Serena and a card Serena had given her.

Patricia put the newspaper into the drawer and closed it carefully. Then she glanced at her watch. It was time to go to the university's Counseling Center, where she'd made an appointment. She'd decided she wanted some help dealing with Serena's death, and it was time to get started.

Tony Ferguson, too, kept a copy of the article about Troy Brinkman's arrest. He pasted it carefully into the scrapbook he'd made about Serena, and then smiled a little. Serena was dead, but she would always be there for him. Besides, there were other women, anyway. Today, in fact, he was going to interview Caroline Shaw, a gifted tennis player who was on her way to national competition. He liked Caroline already.

When Tessa Oliver read the news of Troy's arrest, she couldn't feel anything but a sense of loss about Serena's death and dismay about its effect on her own life. Troy had ruined her Tilton experience. So had Marcie Bratton. In fact, at the end of the semester, Tessa would be transferring to the large state university a few hours to the west. She could no longer imagine staying here.

After he read the news about Troy's arrest, Jesse Montgomery put the paper away and prepared to go to his appointment at the Center of Hope, a local community center. There, he gave free violin lessons to area schoolchildren whose families couldn't afford to pay. It was part of the agreement his lawyer had made with the D.A.'s office. He would perform this community service until he'd completed his requirement. He'd been there a few times already and was beginning to think it wasn't so bad. He would be in debt for a few years because of the attorney fees, court costs and restitution costs, and he would feel a sense of humiliation for the rest of his life. He would always have his arrest and conviction on his record. But he also had the feeling that it could all have been much, much worse. He had tenure, so although he had a formal censure in his record, his Faculty Senate representative had been able to work with him and the administration to negotiate an agreement that would allow him to stay at Tilton. He didn't have the Amati, but he had his life.

That afternoon, Marcie Bratton prepared to lead her brigade in their daily drills. Ever since she'd been removed as RA, she'd tried to throw herself more and more into her military activities. She still burned with anger whenever she thought about Patricia Stanley and Tessa Oliver. How dare they get her kicked out of her job? But she was smart enough to know that she would have to bide her time. She'd been formally warned by the Dean of Students that her conduct would be watched, and that if anything else happened, she might be asked to leave Tilton. So she'd gotten another dorm room and focused on her ROTC work. As angry as the whole situation made her, Marcie also felt a sense of safety. No matter what else happened, at least nobody in ROTC knew her secret, and as long as Patricia Stanley and Tessa Oliver kept their mouths shut, nobody would.

That evening, the Young Artists' Orchestra was just finishing up its first performance. The orchestra had agreed to present three local performances before beginning its tour. Michelle Park had played the last notes of her violin solo. Now the audience responded with thunderous applause. Michelle bowed in acknowledgement and scanned the faces in the first few rows of the audience. There were her parents, with smiles of satisfaction on their faces. Finally, at least for the moment, they approved.

As the audience left after the orchestra's performance, they passed through the lobby of Lessner Hall, where there would soon be a new glass display case. The university had approved the case to display a beautiful Amati violin donated by Spencer and Natalie Brinkman in memory of their daughter, Serena.

About the Author

Margot Kinberg is a mystery novelist with many years of experience in higher education. Don't miss her other Joel Williams, novels, *Publish or Perish* and *Past Tense!* Connect with Margot at her official web site or on Facebook or Twitter.

www.ingramcontent.com/pod-product-compliance
Lightning Source LLC
Chambersburg PA
CBHW070724280626
47159CB00023B/2605